Readers love
STEPHEN OSBORNE

Dead End

"…this latest installment was a winner."

—Boys in our Books

"The love story is really beautiful…"

—It's About The Book

"It has everything a good read needs—characters with interesting personalities, a little angsty romance, good friends, action and danger, all within a well written and paced plot."

—Literary Nymphs Reviews

The Scarlet Tide

"A fun, sarcastic, interesting and quirky detective series that I thoroughly enjoy."

—Gay List Book Reviews

Pale as a Ghost

"This book was funny, bloody, suspenseful, and a really good love story. The love story is left open for future books which I didn't mind because I can't imagine it being tied up neatly."

—Live your Life, Buy the Book

By STEPHEN OSBORNE

Cuddling (Dreamspinner Anthology)
Pop Goes the Weasel • Rat Bastard
Speaking of Dreams
Temporal Driftwood
Wrestling with Jesus

DUNCAN ANDREWS THRILLERS
Pale as a Ghost
Animal Instinct
The Scarlet Tide
Dead End
Under a Blood-red Moon

Published by DREAMSPINNER PRESS
www.dreamspinnerpress.com

UNDER A
BLOOD-RED
MOON

STEPHEN OSBORNE

Published by
DREAMSPINNER PRESS

5032 Capital Circle SW, Suite 2, PMB# 279, Tallahassee, FL 32305-7886 USA
www.dreamspinnerpress.com

Under a Blood-red Moon
© 2016 Stephen Osborne.

Cover Art
© 2016 Anne Cain.
annecain.art@gmail.com
Cover content is for illustrative purposes only and any person depicted on the cover is a model.

ISBN: 978-1-63477-223-5
Digital ISBN: 978-1-63477-224-2
Library of Congress Control Number: 2016901405
Published May 2016
v. 1.0

Printed in the United States of America
∞

This paper meets the requirements of
ANSI/NISO Z39.48-1992 (Permanence of Paper).

For David Haag. Finally.

PROLOGUE

PHIL DAHL was slightly drunk.

Okay, maybe more than slightly. He knew enough, though, not to get behind the wheel of his car. Besides, the cool night air would help to clear his head. The bar where he'd spent the evening, a dive called Barney's Old Time Tavern, wasn't far from his cramped apartment. He'd go home, sleep off the Heinekens he guzzled, and return to Barney's in the morning for his car.

Phil stumbled down Tenth Street, a crooked grin on his face. Had he really come on to a guy at a straight bar? Yeah, the guy was by himself and was hot, but he hadn't given Phil any indication that he was interested. The dude was sipping his beer and watching one of the television screens, which was tuned to ESPN. The sound was off, but the folks at Barney's enabled the closed captioning so people could at least read what the commentators were babbling about. Not that it mattered to Phil. He hated sports. But he did like the looks of the muscular dude sitting on his own at a table.

The guy was big and had a neatly trimmed beard and mustache. He wore a blue tank top, which not only showed off his tattoos, but also his brawn. Phil himself was thin as a rail, but his taste in men ran to athletic types, especially bodybuilders. And this guy obviously spent quite a lot of time in the gym.

So when Phil passed the guy's table on his way back from the restroom, he brazenly stopped and stared at the dude's chest.

The guy shifted his gaze from the tennis highlights on TV to Phil. "Something wrong, bub?" he asked.

The tone wasn't welcoming, but Phil was a little too inebriated to notice. "Just trying to read the tattoo on your chest. Your shirt covers up some of the words."

The guy narrowed his eyes, and Phil thought at first he wasn't going to reply. Finally he growled, "It says Full Moon Rising."

"Oh yeah. I can see that now. Interesting. Is there a story behind that? I mean, it's not the usual phrase people have tattooed on themselves." Phil swayed a little and grabbed hold of the chair opposite the guy to steady himself.

"Yeah." The guy's eyes went back to the tennis.

"Yeah?"

The tattooed man sighed deeply. "Yeah, there's a story." He drank some of his beer and kept his eyes glued to the screen.

Phil was aware he was being dismissed, but as he'd already made contact, he wasn't about to give up without one last effort. Maybe the guy just needed things spelled out. "Can I buy you a beer?"

"Got one."

Phil knew he should just return to his seat, but the thought of going down on this stud's cock—a situation that was looking more and more unlikely—made Phil throw all caution to the wind. "Anything else I can do?" He leaned across the table, his face offering joys that were there for the taking. "I mean, you're here on your own. No babes in this place tonight. If you're wanting to get off…."

Well, there was no harm in suggesting, was there?

The young man glared at Phil with disdain. "Not interested. I suggest you get lost, and quickly."

"Hey, man, just trying to be friendly. I'm pretty good, if I do—"

And then the guy slowly stood. God, he was tall. And big. He dwarfed Phil. Too bad he was a jerk.

Scowling, the dude asked, "Is there something about me that made you think I'd be interested?"

"Well, you were by yourself—"

"Maybe I just wanted to be on my own. Now if I was you, I'd beat it. Before I beat you."

So Phil returned to his seat to grab his jacket. It took a moment to actually put it on, as somehow his left arm seemed unable to get into the appropriate sleeve, but he managed it in the end. His ears felt like they were burning, and he knew he was flushed with embarrassment. Yeah, he was brazen, and he shouldn't have come on to the guy like that, but the dude didn't have to be such an ass about it. Homophobic prick!

And now Phil was five blocks from his home, and he was cold (his damn jacket was too thin!), and he was still horny as hell. Should he find another bar and try again? There weren't any gay bars in the area, most of them being downtown, but even if he was sober enough to drive to one, he didn't have enough gas, and he spent most of his dough on Heinekens.

No, best to go home and watch some porn. As usual.

Phil turned the corner, wishing he could afford to live in a better neighborhood. This area was getting more and more dangerous with gangs and drugs and crack houses and whatever. Hell, there had been three break-ins on Phil's block recently, and one of Phil's friends had a car stolen just last week.

Phil's eyes scanned the shadows for anyone who might be lurking behind a bush or tree, ready to spring out and accost him. The street seemed quiet, though. He could hear someone's television playing too loudly and the sound of light traffic on Tenth behind him, but nothing else. No, he should be safe enough. Besides, what would a mugger get out of him? A couple of bucks at best. Still, anyone holding him up might get mad and retaliate by beating the crap out of him. Phil quickened his pace.

He mapped out the fastest route in his mind. Yes, if he kept to the streets, he could keep to lighted areas, but it would take longer. If he took the shortcut across the vacant lot and through the park, he'd be home in no time. Granted, he'd be stumbling around in the dark, but surely no one would be hanging around the park at this time of night.

Damn, though, that vacant lot looked spooky in the moonlight. The closest house was vacant as well, and had been for ages. The windows were boarded up, and the grass had grown so tall that the For Sale sign was nearly obscured. In this light it looked like something out of a horror movie, a place where ghosts dwelt. Phil decided to give the building a wide berth and began to cross the lot closer to the fence, behind which was an alley and the backs of several businesses.

Something ahead of him darted away, and Phil almost jumped out of his skin before he realized it was only a cat. The animal quickly disappeared, probably off to search the trash of the nearby Chinese restaurant. If so Phil wished the cat luck. He'd eaten there several times, and the food wasn't edible *before* it became trash.

Phil thought he heard a twig snap behind him, as if someone were following him.

He turned quickly but saw nothing. He could still hear that television. The house in question must have every window open for the sound to travel so well. Farther in the distance, a siren wailed. Phil's heart beat faster as he imagined every shadow contained some crack addict, ready to jump him for whatever spare change they could beat out of him. Phil forced himself to go on, but he walked faster through the overgrown grass.

The small hairs on the back of his neck bristled as he heard what sounded like someone breathing. It sounded close, and Phil nearly fell over as he spun around to confront whoever it was.

What was that shadow by the tree? Was something or someone standing there?

He held his breath and stood still, now feeling sober as a judge. "Who's that?" he asked. "Who's there?"

There was, of course, no answer.

Phil took two steps backward, not taking his eyes off the shadow. He reached his hand into his pocket and took out his keys. It wasn't much, but if he spread them out between his fingers, they might make a sort of brass knuckles. Maybe his pursuer was just as nervous as he was, and the thought of getting gouged across the cheek might make them think twice.

But then the shadow moved, and Phil knew no weapon he possessed would frighten off this attacker. It was huge, moving on all fours like a dog. No dog Phil had ever seen was this big, though. A bear, perhaps. Or....

A wolf. But no wolf could be so large.

Phil didn't have time to ponder the impossibility. The thing was leaping at him, and all he could see was a dark shape and slavering jaws. All he could hear now was the monster's growl as it collided with him. The weight of the beast knocked Phil off his feet, and he screamed as he tried in vain to keep the sharp fangs away from his throat.

His scream was cut short as the wolf sank its teeth into Phil's neck. In moments the animal had ripped away skin, muscle, and sinew, leaving Phil's neck a bloody mess. And then the beast began to claw away at Phil, tearing at his chest and stomach.

Minutes later a tall, muscular, and very naked man stepped back over to the tree where he'd left his clothing. By the light of the moon, he donned his jeans and his tight blue tank top, all the while listening to ensure that no one had heard Phil's dying scream. If they had, apparently no one cared. There were no police sirens coming toward the lot, and no one in the nearby houses was coming out to investigate.

As the man slipped on his shoes, balancing against the tree for support, he looked over to the area where Phil lay. The body wasn't visible, the grass was so high. "Well," the man growled, "that was easier than I thought it would be."

Finally dressed again, the man retraced his steps back to Tenth Street. He'd have another beer before heading home.

MAUD BETZ awoke with a start. It took her a moment to realize she was sitting in her chair before the television and not in her bed upstairs. Of course, she'd fallen asleep watching Stephen Colbert while waiting for Graig to show. And it was the sound of the front door that roused her, even though the person entering was attempting stealth.

"Graig?" she asked, sitting up straighter in her armchair. "Is that you?"

"Of course it's me, Grandma."

Graig Betz showed himself in the doorway, looking a bit sheepish and a bit annoyed he hadn't managed to sneak in without getting caught. He was such a handsome young man, Maud thought, although she could do without that mustache of his. Really, it looked like something that old horror movie actor wore. What was his name? Vincent Price!

Yes, Graig probably grew it to look older, but Maud believed it made him look shifty.

And shifty was just what her grandson was being lately. Maud was a small woman with dark skin that was becoming more wrinkled with every year, but she squared her shoulders and treated Graig to her fiercest gaze. "I thought you were going to be home for dinner tonight."

"I worked late" was Graig's tame reply.

"The shop closes at six," she said, standing. "It's now nearly midnight. Just what have you been doing all night? You could have called so that I wouldn't worry."

Graig lowered his gaze. "I was out with the guys."

"You've been spending too much time with them." Maud sniffed. "There's something about them I don't like."

"They're okay, Grandma."

Maud snorted. "They're hooligans, if you ask me." Part of her wanted to berate him more, but he looked so contrite and dejected standing there in the doorway, so she softened her tone. "Have you eaten?"

"Yeah. We ate some burgers."

Maud was tired of speaking to Graig from across the room, so she walked over to him and grabbed hold of his chin with her frail hand. "You look tired," she said, turning his head so it was in better light.

"I'm okay. Really I am."

It didn't sound like it. Maud knew something was troubling Graig. He was always a good kid despite losing his parents at such a young age. While he hadn't thrived in school, he at least kept away from drugs and was never one to get into fights. Now, as a young man, Maud thought Graig was finally finding his way in life. But then he started working with that Brandon Lewis and his crew.

"You're working too much," Maud said. "Why don't you take a day or two off? It'll do you good. You're looking thin."

Graig forced a smile. "Can't afford to, Grandma."

She knew when she was being lied to, especially by her grandson. "What is it?" she demanded. "What's wrong?"

Graig gazed down at his feet. "I... I just... I don't know." With a face full of misery, he looked up into her eyes. "Sometimes I think I've gotten myself into something I can't handle."

Alarm bells went off in Maud's head. "They're not selling drugs down there at that shop, are they?"

Graig managed a weak smile. "You always leap right to drugs. No, it's not that. It's… I don't know. Maybe the auto shop isn't the best place for me to work."

Maud crossed her arms with finality. "Then you quit. There are plenty of jobs out there. You don't have to work where you're not happy."

They both knew jobs were scarce, especially for a young black man with little education and few skills. Graig shook his head sadly. "Don't worry about it, Grandma. I'll work things out."

He gave her a soft peck on the cheek and turned to the staircase, obviously intending to head up to his bedroom. He stopped, however, with his foot on the first step, and glanced back at Maud.

"The thing is, Grandma, I'm not sure I can."

Maud started to speak but stopped when she realized she really didn't know what to say. She watched Graig slowly trudge up the stairs, her face taut with worry. She placed a hand on the banister and closed her eyes, praying for her grandson to find happiness.

She sniffed and detected an odd scent in Graig's wake. An ephemeral smell, there and now gone. But it had a musky tang.

Almost like that of an animal.

CHAPTER 1

I WAS in a bad mood.

Which wasn't good news for the demon I was tracking.

It had actually been quite a while since I was in a bad mood, so in a weird way I was kind of enjoying the experience. Sort of like how one tended to listen to sad music when you were already down in the dumps. Sometimes you just wanted to wallow in your self-pity, at least for a while. This was the same, except I was planning just how dead I was going to make this demon when I found him. And I was going to make him very, very dead.

I was in a storeroom of a department store on the north side of town. It was after midnight, and luckily for me, the store didn't employ a night watchman because I had to break in. Also luck for the night watchman because, if they had one, he'd be demon chow by now.

The place was big, but not so big I shouldn't have run across a Big Nasty by now. I was toward the end of an aisle, surrounded by boxes on shelves reaching almost up to the ceiling, which, considering the ceiling wasn't really all that high, wasn't really impressive. The place was dusty and, as far as I could tell, empty.

This was odd because the Finder spell Gina had cast for me led me directly to the side door of the department store.

I turned the corner, feeling in my bones I was close to my prey. In doing so I nearly ran right into a big yellow-skinned demon with horns, shaggy brown hair, and cigarette breath. We both jumped.

The demon put a hand on his chest as if to keep his heart from jumping out of his body. "Jesus," he growled. "You startled me!"

"I startled you?" I demanded. "You nearly made me pee myself, Elton!"

"My name," he snarled, "isn't Elton."

This was true. I just called him that because of a vague resemblance he bore to the "Crocodile Rock" singer. "Yeah," I said, "but I probably can't pronounce it."

"Is that my fault?"

"Well, you could put a vowel or two in there, make it a little easier. Until then you're Elton."

Elton let this pass. He narrowed his eyes and looked around the darkened room. "I don't think the Byzroth is here."

"No kidding." We were speaking loud enough to alert any demon in the room to our presence. "He must have gone on into the store."

"Why would he do that?"

"I don't know. Maybe he wanted to do some shopping. You tell me. This is your demon hunt."

Earlier that morning I was in the middle of enjoying my first vacation in over a decade with my lover, Robbie. We had a fantastic day planned full of sand, surf, and one hell of a lunch at Captain Curt's Crab and Oyster Bar, not to mention a lot of making out in our hotel room and possibly some on the beach as well. Screw the tourists. But my stay in Siesta Key was cut short by a call from Elton. My first instinct was to tell him to go to Hell, which, considering he was born there, probably wouldn't be the insult I intended. But when Elton informed me Byzroth demons were running amok in Indianapolis, I agreed to hop on the next plane back home. Robbie wanted to come with me, but I insisted he stay and that I'd fly back down as soon as I could. After all, we had the hotel booked for another four days.

I mean, I couldn't let Byzroth demons run amok in my hometown. They're smelly.

Byzroths are sort of the lower class in the demon hierarchy, mainly because they're really, really stupid. They can't talk unless you consider grunting communication, and they have the tendency to kill people with little or no provocation. Basically they're a slave race. They exist, as far as I can tell, to do the dirty work for more evolved demons who don't like to get their hands dirty. I'm no expert on Hell, never having been there, but I'm guessing the Powers That Be needed someone to clean up Hell's restrooms, so they invented Byzroths. Because—believe me—as bad as most demons smell, their excrement is even worse.

The question was, what were Byzroths doing rampaging around Indianapolis? And who were they working for? Let's face it. Some Byzroth demon hadn't been looking through travel brochures and decided to take the family to Indiana for a lovely vacation. True, there was a jazz festival going on, but Byzroths have never really shown much interest in music. No, someone brought them here. And I needed to find out who. Whom. Or what.

I patted Elton's considerable shoulder with my right hand. My left was holding a sword. "So tell me," I said, "what's your angle here?"

He seemed surprised by the question. "I told you. I've got a score to settle."

"Yeah, I know what you told me. They killed a pal of yours. Herman, I think you said. Who's Herman?"

"Is this really the time to go into it?"

Elton frowned, and believe me, he was a good frowner.

"If I'm supposed to blindly go after a pack of Byzroths, yeah, I think I need to know why I'm doing it. For all I know, this is all a scam, and you and your buddies are planning on having me for lunch."

"Please." He seemed insulted. "If I was going to kill you, you'd be mincemeat by now."

"Be that as it may, who's Herman?"

Elton lowered his gaze as he muttered, "He was my pet."

There was another word after pet, but with his grumble, it was hard to make it out.

"What? Cat? Dog? What?"

"Do I look like the kind of demon who would have a cat?"

He had a point. Eat one, maybe. As a pet, no. "So what was Herman?"

"My rat."

I almost dropped the sword. "You got me on a plane out of sunny Florida to avenge a fucking rat?"

"Hey, I loved that little guy!"

Truth be told, he really did look miserable.

"Came home one day and found Herman on the grass outside of my place, a Byzroth standing over him. Fucker didn't even have the decency to eat him whole. I gutted the bastard, of course, but then I realized he wasn't alone. There were about three of them, hiding in the bushes. I barely got out alive myself."

"What the hell are you doing back in Indianapolis, anyway? Last I heard you were in Paris. Thanks for the postcard, by the way."

"You're welcome, and I ran out of money. What did you expect? It's not exactly like I can get a job at a Dairy Queen, what with these horns sticking out of my head."

"I don't know," I muttered. "I've seen worse working there." I paused, partially because I was allowing my eyes to adjust to the gloom, and partially because I didn't want to annoy a demon by asking my next question. "Um, I hate to point this out, but... don't you guys... um... well, *eat* rats?" It was a fair question as, generally, anything with a pulse was lunch to a demon.

Luckily I didn't get hatred vibes coming off Elton, although he did sniff angrily.

"Not for me. Vegetarian now."

A vegetarian demon? "Now I've heard everything," I muttered.

"Well, with the exception of a wino every now and then. You can't go cold turkey on these things."

I thought I saw someone out of the corner of my eye and turned quickly, brandishing my trusty katana, which was a gift from my father back when I was a teen and he was still alive. I'm pretty sure he never foresaw a time I'd actually use it. The figure, however, didn't jump back in fright from the sight of my blade. In fact, it didn't move at all. Statues rarely did.

Actually at first I thought it was a mannequin. After all, we were in a department store stockroom. But this thing was gray, and when I got close enough to touch it, there was a grainy feel to the surface. Definitely stone. "Why would someone stick a statue here?" I asked.

"Who cares?" Elton was itching for a fight, and statues didn't interest him.

I shrugged, although the effigy still bothered me. Why would anyone have a statue in the middle of a storeroom? And there wasn't anything special about the subject either. It wasn't Abraham Lincoln or the Venus de Milo, just some dude who looked like he was out for a stroll. There was a look of surprise on the guy's face, like he just turned a corner and saw something that shocked him to the core. He wasn't even a particularly handsome subject. Oh well. There was no accounting for taste. What did I know about art?

Elton and I continued on our way, but we didn't get very far. The sound of our voices must have carried because as soon as we got about twenty feet away from the double doors I assumed led into the department store, all hell broke loose. The doors crashed open and a horde of Byzroths came dashing through, and they didn't look like they wanted to invite us to tea. They were growling and slobbering and howling, their eyes red with bloodlust.

Elton rushed forward and grabbed one of them. He didn't need a katana, as his hands, already basically claws, became even fiercer when he was riled. The nails grew and sharpened in seconds, much to the dismay of the poor Byzroth, who found his throat slit before he even got to raise his hands in defense. Elton tossed him aside and two others jumped him.

There were about eight Byzroths total, although I didn't really stop to take a head count. One charged at me, screaming out a Byzroth war cry, and I slashed my sword across his chest before he had a chance to get too uppity with me. He was wearing a grimy black robe, a garment highly favored by Byzroths, and I think I mostly got fabric. Still, he wasn't happy with me, and he lunged again. I got him right in the neck on my backswing.

While I was concentrating on him, another one came up and grabbed me by the right elbow, obviously with the intent of disarming me. He dug his claws into my flesh, but I barely noticed my shirtsleeve was now being dyed with my own blood. I jerked my arm free, trying to ignore the searing pain as his nails raked my skin, and spun on my heels, slashing the blade with all my might. His head went rolling.

The first Byzroth that attacked me came back for seconds, even though his neck was gushing black demon blood. He howled as I pierced his chest. Just to make sure he was dead, I buried the blade in far enough that the tip came out of his back. A cool move, but as he fell, his body wanted to take the blade down with him, and I had to struggle to extract it as the Byzroth slumped to the floor.

Luckily for me the battle was actually over. While I was dealing with my two, Elton ripped the others to pieces, and their bodies were lying in heaps around him, staining the floor with blood. There were dismembered arms, legs, and heads all around, and I couldn't help but feel sorry for the poor bastard who'd have to clean up after us. Maybe I should call Merry Maids, just to see how they'd react.

I cradled my wounded arm to my chest. "Damn it, this was a new shirt too."

"Duncan! There's another one!"

I was too busy examining the carnage to notice another figure had slipped through the door. This one was tiny compared to the Byzroths we slaughtered and was moving fast. I couldn't see much, as the figure was wearing a hooded cloak and was keeping to the shadows. I did a fancy jump over dead Byzroth number one and caught up with the newcomer, who growled as they realized the jig was up. As the figure turned, I swung, aiming at the neck. The head would have gone flying if it weren't for the pulled-up hood. The body collapsed and the now-detached head rolled free.

It wasn't a Byzroth, and I think the only thing that saved me was the fact it was so damned dark in that area of the storeroom that I really couldn't get a good look at the head. What I did see chilled my blood. The demon I just killed was a female, and she had snakes in her hair, which were still writhing as they died.

"What the hell?" I asked. Even as the snakes breathed their last, I found it hard to look at them but impossible to look away. It was as if, even dying, they were trying to steal my very soul. I was transfixed, unable to move. When the last snake finally stopped moving, I swallowed hard and realized I could blink once more. I looked at Elton, who was looking down on the dead woman with awe.

"I think you just killed Stheno," he said softly.

"Who?" I asked.

He looked at me, eyes wide.

"Stheno. One of the Gorgons."

"That would explain the snakes. Like Medusa, huh? *Clash of the Titans* and all that?"

Elton shook his head. "You don't understand. She's supposed to be immortal."

I shoved the body a little with my foot. "Doesn't seem too immortal right now." The head bothered me, though. The black eyes seemed to stare up at me, as if saying, "You'll pay for this, you katana-wielding bastard."

I was being flip with Elton, but the truth was I felt like hell. I wanted nothing more than to go home and crawl into bed and sleep for a week. The sword in my hand felt heavy as heck, and my eyelids were drooping.

"What's a Gorgon doing in Indianapolis, anyway?" I asked. "And why the small army of Byzroths?"

"I don't know," Elton answered. "The Gorgons haven't been heard from in centuries. Whatever she was planning, she must have summoned these Byzroths to do the dirty work."

"Well, whatever she was planning," I said, "I don't think she's going to…."

I dropped the katana and realized I was swaying. The room was spinning, or maybe it was just my head. I would have collapsed right next to Stheno on the floor if Elton hadn't caught me.

"You don't look so hot," he said, easily holding my weight against his chest.

"My phone," I muttered. "Call Gina."

Things went black after that.

CHAPTER 2

I AWOKE with Excedrin Headache Number 216, which I think covers having seen a Gorgon in its death throes.

My eyelids felt heavy, but they worked. I opened them to slits, not wanting to overwork the little bastards. I seemed to be in my bedroom, in my bed, and a small young woman with long black hair was standing over me, a bemused smile on her face.

"Well," she said, "we got in a little over our head this time, didn't we?"

"What happened?" I asked. I'm pretty sure it came out "Wah havvah?" I rubbed my forehead as if that would quell the fire raging within my skull. It didn't.

The woman was sitting in a chair she'd placed next to the bed. She leaned back, her legs crossed. "Well, you left your lover down in Florida so that you could rush back here and play superhero. Then you brazenly attacked a horde of demons, one of whom slashed your arm up pretty good, and you topped off the evening by chopping off the head of a Gorgon. You saw her as she was dying, so that's why you collapsed. Seconds earlier and you'd have been a nice Duncan Andrews statue that the pigeons could have shit on to their hearts' content. As it is your muscles just froze up a little and you've got a migraine."

Gina's a good best friend to have, as she's a healing witch. Well, she's a good best friend for *me* to have, as I always seem to be getting maimed, shot, or generally broken. In her current guise, she appeared to be a woman in her early twenties, but in actuality, she was hundreds of years old.

I took in a deep breath and tried speech again, this time with more success. "How was I to know she was a Gorgon? Really, these demons need to wear name tags or something."

She ignored me and went on.

"I healed the damage to your muscles with a little liniment. Special concoction of mine. Of course I could have gotten rid of your headache easily, but I thought I'd let you keep that for abandoning Robbie."

And here she smacked me on the arm.

"You stupid shit!"

"I was only going to be gone one night. Then I was coming back!"

It sounded lame even to me. I mean, I spent over ten years moping because my boyfriend was dead, and I get him back, and what do I do but skedaddle right in the middle of our first vacation together since he came back to life. Hear me out, though. He got us tickets to a Taylor Swift concert. I mourned Robbie when he died at the age of twenty, accepted it when he stuck around as a ghost for the next decade, and rejoiced when, miraculously, he came back to life. In my time I've killed to protect him. I've been beaten and pummeled, stabbed, slashed, and even bitten, but I've always been there for him. I draw the line, however, at Taylor Swift.

Actually I'd have gone to the concert and probably enjoyed it because I could endure anything just to see him smile, but when Elton called, he made it seem like Indianapolis was crawling with Byzroths, and if someone didn't do something, we'd have demons everywhere. How was I to know he was overreacting because of a dead rat? And I really did intend to be back as soon as possible, and Robbie assured me he'd be fine on his own.

"Dunc," he said as he left me off at the airport in our rental car, "I love you, but since I've come back, you've hardly left my side for a second. Go. Kill demons. I'll be fine on my own. I haven't been on my own in ages. Not as a human, anyway."

And so I went. Now I was regretting my decision. "What time is it?" I asked.

Gina looked at the clock on the wall. "Just about seven."

I groaned. "I hate mornings."

"That's fine because it's evening."

I sat up quickly, which was a mistake. My head felt like someone detonated TNT inside it. I grasped my temples in a vain attempt to keep my brain from oozing out my ears. I was mildly surprised when it didn't, but I did let out a good-sized howl of pain. "You mean I've been asleep for nearly a day?"

"Sit back," Gina commanded, her helpful hands on my shoulders.

Once my head was back on the pillow, she pried my fingers from my temples and placed her own there. She rubbed gently while reciting some incantation. The migraine vanished completely.

"Don't worry. I've talked to Robbie. He's fine. I told him that his lover is an ignorant, stupid man-child who should never be left alone because he's too pigheaded to know when he's in over his head, and he of course agreed with me. I told him to stay down there and enjoy himself. He went to Disney World today. He said he'd bring you back mouse ears."

A pang of regret stabbed my heart. I really had wanted to experience the theme park with him, but it served me right for thinking I had to protect the city I lived in from every nasty creature that roamed its streets. "Well," I grumbled, "at least I avenged Herman's death."

Gina blinked. "Excuse me?"

"Just some rat that met its end due to the Byzroths." I sat up again. This time there were no cranial explosions. I noted I was wearing only a pair of shorts and wondered who changed my clothes. I figured it was Gina. Elton would have been too shy. "So," I said, "a Gorgon. I didn't know they were real."

"I knew they were real," Gina said with a shrug. "I just thought they were all dead. No one's heard from them in ages. Leave it to you to find one in a department store." She rose and went over to the bedroom door, which she opened. "There's someone here who's been dying to see you, by the way."

There was a flurry of motion and loads of plaintive and reproachful barks as Daisy, my bulldog, scrambled into the room. In seconds she was in my arms, licking me with her disturbingly dry tongue between yelps of joy.

In my topsy-turvy world, everything seemed to change if I wait around long enough. My beloved Robbie was dead but now was back.

Gina used to look vastly different from the way she looks now. The one fixed point in my life is Daisy. Oh sure, she might be dead and a zombie, and she might have a grayish tint to her skin and red eyes and she bites the heads off squirrels, but she's always been there to cheer me up.

In fact, when Robbie had suggested a vacation, my only pang of regret was we'd have to leave Daisy behind, albeit in the capable hands of Gina. What with work and dead boyfriends and demons and vampires and what have you, I'd not ventured far from the borders of the city in over a decade, so Daisy was used to me being there on a day-to-day basis. She watched with a seemingly worried look as Robbie and I packed for our trip, and by the time we were ready to leave, I could see resentfulness mixed with fear in her eyes. Walking out of the door while Gina held her was the hardest thing I've had to do in ages.

The reunion, though, was worth all the angst. Daisy's tongue became a weapon, and she unleashed it on my chin, lips, nose, and even my eyelids. I let her have free rein until I couldn't take it any longer and pulled her off my face. It took some force, but I finally got her onto my lap.

"I missed you too, Daisy," I said. The sound of my voice caused her to attempt another attack, but I held her in place.

"Nick was by earlier," Gina said, still standing by the doorway. "He said he'd come back when you weren't dead to the world. Apparently he's got news."

"Yeah?" Nick was a good friend. At one point he could have made me change my relationship status on Facebook from "Single, but I have a boyfriend that's a ghost that's still around but I can't touch" to "It's complicated." I quickly realized, though, that tempting as Nick was, Robbie was the love of my life, dead, living, or pickled in aspic. Since then Nick's become a fixture in my life, a trusty friend and compatriot.

"He didn't elaborate. Just said news."

Knowing Nick, it would be that he finally decided to remodel his kitchen, a project we'd heard about for months now even though no actual work commenced beyond leafing through magazines. Maybe he bought a faucet. I was spared further thoughts of Nick's kitchen by the ringing of my phone.

I knew it was my phone because it was next to me on the nightstand, but the ringtone had been changed, so now I was hearing Bon Jovi's "You Give Love A Bad Name." I glared at Gina, who had the decency to nearly look contrite.

"Sorry," she said. "I zapped it. Seemed appropriate."

Worse, the caller was Robbie. It was like the two of them planned the moment just to make me feel more like a heel than I already did. I answered. "I thought you were going to Disney World today."

"I'm there." Robbie sounded breathless and excited, which he often did nowadays. He was finding living again a marvelous experience, and who could blame him? "Standing outside Cinderella's Castle. Just rode the Haunted Mansion for the second time. Boy, did they get that wrong. They should have consulted actual ghosts when they built that thing."

"Yeah, I'm sure it would have made the ride so much better." I wanted so badly to be there with him, but he seemed to be enjoying himself. Why oh why did I have to get on that plane? Why did I feel like I had to be the one to vanquish all the nasties that set foot in Indianapolis? Couldn't the Byzroth threat have waited a few days?

Well, yes. But a Gorgon running around town? No, that wouldn't do. I did the right thing coming back. Saved some lives, saved some people being turned into stone. Still, I wished I could be with Robbie in the Magic Kingdom.

"So Gina tells me you've been busy," Robbie said.

I could hear happy people around him, plus joy in his voice.

"Chopping heads off Gorgons, huh? Isn't that big-time stuff?"

"Yeah, comes with consequences too. My legs feel like they're made of lead."

"That may just be that you're getting older. I noticed at the beach the other day that your knees are getting knobby."

"My knees are so not knobby."

"They'll do until something knobbier comes along."

I was feeling tons better just from hearing Robbie's voice. I could almost feel the love coming through the phone. "So what's next? The Small World ride?"

"Fuck no! I'd never be able to get that damned song out of my head. I'm thinking the Hall of Presidents, or maybe the Country Bear Jamboree. You know, the classics."

"Have fun. I'm about to check flights. I'll be back with you ASAP."

His voice lost a little of the lighthearted tone. "So what was a Gorgon doing in Indianapolis?"

"Don't know. Whatever it was, I'm sure it wasn't anything good." Suddenly the picture of the carnage Elton and I left in the department store storeroom flashed in my head. I could just imagine what the staff thought when they arrived for their morning shift. Black goo everywhere and lifeless Byzroths littering the floor, not to mention a beheaded Gorgon. Normally I'd have cleaned up the mess I made—possibly just by burning the joint to the ground—but I'd not been in any condition for mopping up. Which meant—

I must have had a premonition because just then there was a pounding on my front door. It wasn't a nice pounding either, so I didn't expect it to be a sweet little Girl Scout selling cookies.

"I've got to go," I said as Gina went to answer the door before the guy damaged the wood. Realizing she was getting lax in the home protection department, Daisy sprang off the bed and ran after Gina, barking all the way. I heard a commotion as Gina opened the door. Seconds later Lieutenant David Carson of the Indianapolis Metropolitan Police burst into my bedroom, his face red and his eyes blazing.

Spotting me propped up in bed, he jabbed an accusatory finger my way.

"You...." He was sputtering. "You and your fucking weird shit!"

I did my best to look innocent. "What weird shit would that be?"

Carson looked like he was ready to explode. "Before I throw you in a jail cell and throw away the key, I'd like you to tell me why I've got a JCPenney store with several dead bodies in it!" He loomed over my bed. "Bodies that aren't human, I might add!"

My innocent look may have faltered a little.

CHAPTER 3

IT TOOK quite a while to get Carson calmed down to the point where he didn't want to punch something, namely me. Finally, with Gina's help, I filled him in on what took place. I'm not sure he believed all of it, but he'd been around me long enough not to dismiss the story outright. In the end we went with him to the scene of the crime. Well, massacre.

The bodies were now covered, and there were remarkably few cops lounging around, which I took to be Carson's doing. He was trying to keep as few people as possible involved. Even so the police officers were keeping as far away from the bodies as they could, especially the decapitated ones. They were writing notes or whispering to each other, anything to keep from looking at the covered Byzroths.

Carson stood in the doorway, shaking his head. "I don't know how I can keep this from getting out. Demons, you say? What are people going to think when they find out there are demons running around the city?"

"Who says they have to know?" I asked politely.

Carson did more sputtering. When he finally got to the point where words came out, he said, "For one thing, the manager and assistant manager came in this morning and found the bodies! And strangely they noticed they were a sickly yellow color and that they had horns growing out of the tops of their heads! Oh, and did I mention the young woman who is lying over there with her head cut off? Once I heard the call, I got this place locked down tight, but even the few officers who have been allowed in are in a state of shock! And who can blame them!"

He narrowed his eyes at me. "I knew as soon as I saw the corpses that somehow you were involved in this!"

"You flatter me, Lieutenant."

"Well, whenever I find fang marks on someone's neck or someone has been devoured by squirrels, I know you're involved in some way, shape, or form!"

"We can take care of this," I assured him. I nodded to Gina. "I don't think you've been properly introduced to my friend here. This is Gina."

Carson frowned in confusion. "Don't you know women with any other name?" he growled.

I could have explained to him this Gina was the same one as the tall blonde person he already knew and she'd just morphed into a new form. After all, it would have been fun to see Carson have a total mental breakdown right in front of a few of his officers, but I restrained myself.

"I can help, Lieutenant," she said with an ingratiating smile.

He didn't look convinced. "That I'd like to see."

Gina's smile grew as she approached the nearest cop, who was pretending to take notes.

"Excuse me, but can I ask your name, Officer?"

"Jenkins," the man replied.

Gina placed a hand on the side of his face. "Forget, Jenkins. Forget what you thought you saw here. What really happened here was a gang fight. These bodies are human, the unfortunate result of a drug deal gone sour."

Jenkins blinked. When Gina removed her hand, he stepped back a pace and then shook his head, as if clearing away mental cobwebs. In doing so he came close to tripping over one of the Byzroth bodies, only being saved by Gina reaching out a hand to steady him.

"Careful," she said.

"Thanks, Miss," he said, blinking rapidly. He let out some air. "Guess I had a dizzy spell there."

"What seems to have happened here, Officer Jenkins?"

Jenkins glanced over at his superior for assistance.

Carson nodded and said, "It's okay, Jenkins. This young lady is helping with the investigation."

Jenkins rubbed his forehead. I'm guessing his brains were still feeling a little cloudy.

"Well, Miss, at a guess, I'd say this was a drug deal gone bad." He glanced around at the covered bodies. "Real bad."

Carson glanced at me and then at Gina and then back to me, eyes wide. "What the hell?"

Gina shrugged. "It's easy, especially when you want them to forget something they'd really like to forget."

Carson lowered his voice conspiratorially. "And you can do this to everyone who's seen this mess? My men, the store workers, everyone?"

"Everyone," Gina replied with a smile.

Now it was Carson's turn to look like he was going to fall backward onto a body, and he hadn't even been zapped. "Oh, my fucking aunt!" he muttered. His face pale, he turned to me. "What is she, some kind of…. I don't know if I even want to say it."

"She's a witch," I said.

"I need to sit down." For a moment it looked like Carson was going to choose one of the dead bodies to plunk down on, but he luckily found a nearby stool he could perch on instead.

Gina went over to him and placed a gentle hand against his cheek. "Forget, my dear Carson," she said. "And sleep."

It was a good thing he was next to a wall, or he'd have slumped off the stool onto the floor. Instead he clunked his head against the plaster as his eyes closed and his mouth went slack.

"Ouch," I said.

"I thought he needed the rest," Gina explained to me. "The man always has dark circles under his eyes."

"Now what?" I asked.

"We do the same for his men, then the workers who found the bodies, and then we clean up this mess. You'd better call your demon friend. This isn't going to be fun." She then strode to the center of the room and clapped her hands to get the attention of Carson's cronies. "Excuse me, guys," she said in a sweet voice. "Can I have a quick word with you?"

I HAVE no idea what Carson believed happened when he woke up. All I know is he didn't call or come bursting in to see me, so he must have come up with some explanation as to why he woke up in a storeroom and there wasn't a massacre like the one that was called in. I only know Elton and I spent a couple of backbreaking hours loading dead Byzroth bodies into a dumpster, which Gina then incinerated. It wasn't your normal, everyday kind of fire either, because when it burned out, there was nothing left. Not even a bone. The dumpster didn't fare too well either.

Once I finally got back home, I was weary, worn out, and I had a big splotch of gooey black demon blood on my shirt. I took Daisy out for a feeding and a poo, and then began to look up flights to Florida. I was sitting on the couch using my laptop, Daisy on one side of me, a glass of wine on the other. It would have been perfect if only Robbie were with us. As soon as I found a flight, though, I'd be back in his arms, and—

There was a knock at the door.

You can tell a lot about how someone knocks. There's a tentative knock, which can be from a neighbor who isn't sure they should be complaining about the bloodcurdling screams coming from your apartment, which has happened to me on occasion. But hey, it's hard to stake a vampire without them making a fuss. There's an authoritative knock, which is usually from a law enforcement official wondering why the neighbors have called about bloodcurdling screams coming from your apartment. There's also the businesslike knock from young people wanting to know if you'd like to see the latest issue of *The Watchtower* and hear about their religion.

And then there's a desperate knock. A knock from someone in trouble. A knock from someone who's at their wits' end, and who has come to the one person in town who won't think they're crazy. A person who needs the services of Duncan Andrews, Private Detective and Monster Killer. I don't put that last part on my business cards. It's just implied.

This was one of those knocks, but I didn't have time. I had to get down to Florida and see my beautiful boyfriend doing high dives in the hotel pool. "Go away!" I said when the knocking persisted. "I'm asleep!"

There was a short pause, like the knocker was pondering this statement. Then they resumed with more vigor.

"I'm not here!" I yelled. "I'm in Des Moines with a sick aunt!"

"I can keep this up all day, Mr. Andrews!" called a muffled voice from the hallway.

You can tell a lot about a person's voice as well. For instance, I knew this person was female, older, and smoked, probably a hell of a lot. She also had chutzpah and wasn't going to take no for an answer. I sighed and looked down at Daisy, who was already annoyed the knocking had disturbed her after-meal snooze.

"So much for Florida," I said to the dog.

I'm not psychic, at least not in the way people generally think of psychics. I can't read minds or tell the future. I just see ghosts and know when there's something supernatural around. Every now and then, though, I do get a premonition. And I was getting one now that told me I wasn't going to be rejoining Robbie down in the Sunshine State.

With a sigh I got up, Daisy at my heels, and went to the door. I opened it to find an old woman standing there, dark of skin, gray of hair, and thin as a rail. She sniffed when she saw me.

"You took your time, young man."

"Sorry about that." I hesitated. If I let her in, I was sending a signal I was willing to listen to whatever she had to pitch me, and therefore there'd be no chance of me joining Robbie. I decided we could transact our business in the doorway. "How can I help you?"

The woman took matters into her own hands and pushed past me. Entering my living room, she sniffed again as she looked around, obviously finding my decorating tastes questionable. Daisy seemed a little taken aback by the woman—I didn't blame her—and scuttled back a few paces to give the old woman some room.

"Your dog is dead," the woman said simply.

That took me by surprise. People often noted Daisy looked sickly or something similar, but no one had previously correctly surmised she was no longer alive. I figured a noncommittal response would be best. "She seems to get around all right, though."

The woman shrugged, dismissing any further discussion about the dog's status. As I closed the door, she said, "I thought you said you were in Des Moines with a sick aunt."

"She got better." I felt like I was being admonished by a stern schoolteacher.

"Do you make it a habit to lie to old women who come to your door?" There was a twinkle in her eyes, and I realized I was in the presence of a master kidder, someone who liked to play with people's perceptions. She also liked to get right to the point. "You have a reputation, Mr. Andrews."

"A good one, I hope."

"People say you're crazy as a bedbug."

"Nice mixed metaphor. Please sit down, Miss...."

"Mrs. Betz. Maud Betz." She sat down in the big armchair. She was so thin three of her could have sat there. With her simple black purse in her lap, she glanced around the apartment again. "You don't have a wife. That's for sure. Nothing feminine about this room." She rested her gaze on Daisy, who had retreated to a corner to eye the woman to make sure she was safe. "Wouldn't it have just been easier to get a new dog, rather than resurrect the old one?"

"Yeah, but then you have to go through potty training all over again. Can I get you something to drink, Mrs. Betz?"

"Call me Maud. And a gin would do nicely. Don't drown it with the tonic."

I assumed she'd want tea or maybe water, and saw by the gleam in her eye she was fully aware she'd scored points with me. I went to the kitchen and fixed us both drinks. When I returned I found she'd gotten up and was checking out my bookshelves and CD collection. She arched an eyebrow when I handed her the gin.

"Neil Diamond?" she asked.

"What can I say? I like a bit of sequins with my music."

"A lot of jazz. I like that. But I'm assuming the Taylor Swifts belong to someone else."

They were Robbie's. "Did you really look me up to discuss my CD collection?"

Maud Betz nodded, accepting the rebuke. "I'm stalling. I know. It's odd, but I know from what I've heard that what I've got to tell you won't come as a shock to you, and I know you won't dismiss me as some sort of kook, but I'm still reluctant to say it aloud."

"Sit down, Mrs. Betz."

She resumed her seat and sipped at the gin. Her face showed approval. Score one for Tanqueray. I sat down on the couch opposite her. Daisy hopped up and sat next to me. She seemed wary of the newcomer, unwilling to take her eyes off Maud for long.

"Obviously you've come to me because something strange has happened either to you or to someone you know." I gave Daisy a good scratch behind the ears as I talked to calm her down. It worked. She lost interest in Maud, did three circles on the couch, and finally lay down. "You've done some research. Actually a lot since you came to my apartment rather than call my office number. My home address isn't on my business cards or in that horribly expensive ad I put in the yellow pages."

"Wasn't easy to find it, let me tell you." Maud finished the gin and looked at the glass as if she were hoping it would refill itself.

"Glad to hear it. I have some people that I'd rather not have access to that information." I sat back. "Let me tell you, there's nothing you can say that will shock me. I once had a woman who came to me and asked me to help look for her leg."

It was a true story. What I didn't tell Maud was the woman was crazy and she had both of her legs attached.

Maud set the glass down on the end table next to her, making sure it went on a coaster. None of those nasty rings. She took in a deep breath and looked me squarely in the eyes.

"It's about my grandson," she said.

"What about him?"

She narrowed her eyes. "I believe he's a werewolf."

CHAPTER 4

"I'LL CATCH the first flight back."

Part of me wanted to agree, tell Robbie to get his keister back to Indy as soon as possible. I missed him horribly. I also didn't want him to cut short the only vacation he'd had in over a decade. Long-distance trips weren't easy for ghosts. Besides, I didn't want to be the party pooper. "Stay where you are," I told him. "We've got the hotel booked for another couple of days. I might be able to get this handled and get back down there."

"What, in time for us to get on a plane and come back home?"

He had a point. Plus there was little chance I'd be able to take care of Mrs. Betz's errant grandson that quickly. For one thing the lad had disappeared. So first I had to find him, then find out if he really was a Furry Nasty, and then decide what to do with him.

I was driving to an Applebee's on the north side to meet with Nick, who was going to fill me in on his big news. After that I planned on hitting up some of Graig Betz's acquaintances to see if I could get a clue as to where he'd gone. Maud had spelled his name for me, wanting to make sure I knew it wasn't the usual Greg. I had my phone plugged in to the car, so I wasn't breaking the law in that respect. Doing sixty in a forty-five zone would get my wrists slapped, though, so I slowed down a tad.

"It's my fault," I said. "I don't want you to suffer. It's not like I *had* to take the case. I could have told her to stuff it or that it had to wait until I got back."

"Yeah, but that wouldn't have been you," Robbie said.

He knew me so well. "So stay. It might even be good for us to be apart from each other for a few days. Just think of the sex when you get back."

"Yeah. We can break another bed." I heard him sigh. "I kind of want to be on this case with you. You need my help."

No, I didn't. He was human now, and vulnerable. He could get hurt, and werewolves had pointy claws. True, I was human as well, but that was different. I wasn't quite sure how, but it was. "The first couple of days are going to be spent tracking this guy down. Boring stuff. By the time I find him and see if he howls at the moon, you'll be back, all nice and suntanned." And I still wouldn't let him help on the case. I had to protect the little bastard now, although I couldn't tell him that.

Robbie still sounded unconvinced. "It's no fun down here without you. I'll come back."

"No fun." I could hear crowds in the background. "You're still at Disney World, aren't you?"

"Yeah, but—"

"And you're telling me the Magic Kingdom isn't fun?"

"Well, it would be more fun with you here."

"We'll go again. And the next time, you'll have the inside scoop and can tell me what rides to avoid."

"Yeah, and someone will call to tell you their husband got eaten by penguins, and you'll head right back."

I was approaching the restaurant. "I won't next time. I promise."

"Uh-huh."

"Penguins?"

"They're not as sweet as they look. That and some guy in line here has a penguin on his shirt, and they were on my mind. I've got to go. I'm almost ready to do Space Mountain. Call me tomorrow."

"Will do."

He rang off, and I felt a pang of regret and loneliness. I really did hate to be away from him, but I also knew we shouldn't be connected at the hip. Robbie had freedom now, and he should enjoy it.

Plus I didn't want him to get ripped to shreds by a werewolf.

I sighed as I pulled into the lot of Applebee's. Sooner or later I was going to have to come to terms with the fact Robbie was no longer a spirit and was now flesh and blood. He was my partner, and it was natural he'd want to accompany me on cases, even the dangerous ones.

I just wasn't sure I could live with myself if anything happened to him.

"Duncan," I said to myself, "you are one contrary bastard."

Contrary and hungry. I trotted quickly inside and told the greeter I was there to meet somebody. She started to ask me for a name, but by that time I'd spotted Nick sitting at a table with some guy I didn't know. Nick waved, and I went to find out what his news was, although I was assuming the news was the guy sitting with him, mainly because before they spotted me, they were holding hands.

Nick looked a little apprehensive, the way one does when introducing a new beau to his friend. It didn't help Nick and I were nearly a couple ourselves, back when I was having trouble with a long-term relationship with a Robbie who was a ghost. And I knew for a long time Nick still had feelings for me, so I was glad to see he'd moved on.

And moved on with a hottie. I'm not good at figuring out ethnicity, and anyway, the lines are often blurred nowadays. This guy may have been a light-skinned black, or maybe Puerto Rican. Hell, he could have been Egyptian for all I knew. I just knew that he was good looking, with short-cropped black hair and eyes that were like dark-brown pools swimming in a sea of white. Best of all was the guy's smile, warm, gentle, and welcoming.

Yeah, I'd have forgotten about me too if I were Nick and met this hunk.

Nick took a deep breath, and I could almost feel him starting to sweat.

"Duncan, I'd like you to meet Casey. Casey Santos, this is Duncan Andrews."

The guy had a good handshake too. He didn't try to crush my fingers in one of those I'm-more-macho-than-you shakes, nor did he hand me a limp fish.

"I've heard a lot about you," he said pleasantly.

"Good things, I hope." We sat, and I couldn't help but grin at Nick. "So what's new?"

Nick was pale, and his hand shook a little as he sipped from his water glass. "Oh, not much. Grading finals. Played some golf over the weekend. Did pretty well. Casey's a little better than me, but I gave him a pretty good game."

Casey patted Nick on the thigh, and I couldn't help but notice he left his hand there.

"Nick's too modest. Do you play golf, Duncan?"

"Me? No. I tried it once. The ball attacked me." Everyone chuckled, Nick uneasily. He wasn't sure whether or not I was kidding. "So," I said, wanting to jump right to the big question, "how long have you two been...."

I should have said "dating," but I didn't want to presume. Then again, by letting the sentence trail, I made it sound like I might have been about to say "fucking." Well, Casey's hand *was* on Nick's thigh, right near the danger zone. I guessed they had gone beyond a handshake and a hearty hello.

Nick flushed, pleased and embarrassed at the same time. "Just over a month now," he said, looking to Casey for confirmation.

"Wow. You've kept it quiet that long? Is it Facebook official yet?"

"Well, you've been busy," Nick said. "And you can't announce that you're dating someone to your friends right away. Jinxes it, you know."

"If you believe in jinxes," Casey said with a laugh.

"Where did you meet?" I asked.

Nick's face was so red, tomatoes were getting jealous. "He sold me my golf clubs."

I didn't even know Nick was into golf. The things you learn. Casey leaned back, finally taking his hand off Nick's leg.

"I work at Dick's Sporting Goods. I'm not normally in the golf department, but I was filling in that day. Otherwise I might have missed out on meeting Nick."

The waitress came and took our orders. Nick stuttered a bit and actually asked for a roasted "garnic sirloin," but the waitress assumed he meant garlic. She went away, and Nick helped himself to more water.

Nick's so nervous. He shouldn't be. I like his friend. Seems like a nice guy. Bit odd, though. Something weird about him.

Okay, that was different. I had, in fact, been thinking Nick should calm down, but the voice in my head wasn't mine. It was like I read someone else's mind for just a second or two, which was a strange feeling. I looked questioningly at Casey, who locked eyes with me.

Oh my God, you heard that, didn't you?

Again, not my voice in my head. It was Casey's. His lips hadn't moved, and he hadn't spoken, but I heard him nonetheless. I wondered if I thought hard enough if he would hear my reply. I tried it. *Yes.*

Casey nodded warily.

Don't say anything. I haven't told Nick yet.

Wow. A conversation without actual words being spoken. Freaky. I concentrated on sending a thought back to Casey. *My lips are sealed.* Which, technically, they were.

Funny. You're a funny guy. I'll explain later. About this.
Okay.

Nick, meanwhile, was making a joke about my aborted vacation. "—should have known you couldn't keep away long. In fact, Robbie bet me you'd only last two days down there before you'd find an excuse to come back."

It was hard to concentrate on someone actually talking when someone else was in your mind. Suddenly, though, it was like the connection between me and Casey was severed, almost as if a door was slammed. I shook my head to clear it and looked at Nick. "Sorry," I said. "I was miles away. What was that?"

Nick repeated what he'd said about Robbie. Just hearing the name made me a little sad and lonely. Robbie was probably currently watching the fireworks show at Disney World. Or did they still do that? "Well," I said, "I made it more than two days."

"Yeah, three."

The waitress and another server came with our food. As his steak was placed in front of him, Casey smiled and said, "Ah, this looks delicious." He flashed me a warning glance, the meaning of which was clear. He would tell me all about his gift in good time. For now we were just three dudes enjoying some food at an Applebee's.

I wondered if he knew Nick could see ghosts and that I killed Nasties for a living. I was betting not.

As the servers walked away, Nick cut into his roasted "garnic sirloin" with gusto.

"I'm surprised Robbie didn't come back with you."

"I made him stay," I said.

Nick snorted. "I doubt that you can make Robbie do anything he really doesn't want to do."

Well, that was true, but it annoyed me Nick said it. I didn't know why. I was already feeling peevish I wasn't with Robbie, so that was my excuse. Still, I shouldn't have done what I did.

As I ate some pasta, I said, "You would pick a restaurant that's haunted."

Nick closed his eyes. "Don't."

Casey was obviously confused. "Haunted?"

I pointed with my fork. "Busboy over there. You probably can't see him. That's okay. Most people can't. Some may see him as a vague mist or a mere shadow, but Nick and I get the full picture. Poor kid's been dead for years, I'm guessing, but he still likes to show up for work every now and then. Steals tips too. Did you notice that, Nick?"

He shook his head. "I hadn't actually got to the big reveal part of the relationship yet."

"That's okay. Casey's got a talent of his own. Mind reading or something like it. Thought transfer? What do you call it, Casey?"

Nick's new beau seemed stunned. "I call it shining. You know, like that Stephen King book. Only works with certain people, though. Works real well with you, I must say. Nick I can't hear at all, which is actually a good thing."

I nodded. "So Nick sees ghosts, and he likes to help them move along to the other side. Me, I kill demons. Well, demons, vampires, and the like. Vanquish nasty spirits. Killed a Gorgon last night. That was something new."

Nick and Casey had stopped eating. They were just staring at me.

And it suddenly came over me I'd just been a horrible ass. To try to make up for it in a tiny way, I smiled at Casey. "So welcome to our little group," I said.

CHAPTER 5

ACCORDING TO his grandmother, Graig Betz worked at a place called Smitty's Autobody on the south side. It was well after ten o'clock by the time I got there, so I didn't expect to find anyone around. There was, however, a light in the window of what I assumed to be the office. The blinds were drawn, but I could see the shadow of someone moving around, so someone was working late. Or robbing the place. Either way my arrival could be interesting.

I parked in the lot and sat with the engine off for a minute or so, watching the movement within. "What do you think, Daisy? Should I go in guns a-blazing and maybe scare the crap out of an elderly cleaning woman?"

Daisy was in the passenger seat, also eyeing the building. I'd collected her after leaving Nick and Casey at Applebee's. The dinner didn't go well after my admittedly rude announcement, but at least they accepted my apology, and we agreed to drop all paranormal talk for the night and just get to know each other. Unfortunately that left little for me to talk about. I whined about Robbie being away and how my mother kept threatening to come for a visit. Nick and Casey, after the meal, went on to find a quiet bar where they could discuss their respective gifts and probably to talk about what a dick I was at dinner. I'd make it up to them later, preferably when Robbie was back and I wasn't in such a shitty mood.

After taking Daisy out for a late-evening snack at the park, I decided to check out Smitty's on a whim. I was glad I had my .38 with me, just in case it wasn't a cleaning woman. I told Daisy, "There are several possibilities. Feel free to bark when you hear the one you think is right. It's a cleaning woman. It's a burglar. It's someone who works there, someone I can ask about Graig Betz. Maybe it's a werewolf, although why he'd be scrounging around a dingy little office is anyone's guess. Hell, it could be Donald Trump." I tapped the gun in its holster. "Oh God, please let it be Donald Trump."

Daisy snorted. I guess she didn't think it was Donald Trump.

"Let's find out, shall we?" I opened the car door and got out, Daisy following.

Just then the light inside went out, and by the time we got to the entrance of Smitty's, someone was coming out. He was a tall guy and very broad. There wasn't a lot of light to go by, but I got the impression he was the body builder type, or maybe his parents were mountain gorillas. Either way, not the sort you wanted to engage in fisticuffs with, not if you like your teeth. Luckily my gun was snuggled against me under the light jacket I donned, making me feel superior. You can bench 415? Well, screw you! I can shoot a beer can at ten yards, which is especially useful if you hate beer cans.

He seemed surprised to find a guy and a dog approaching him. Now that we were closer, I could see he was about my age and had a deep tan, a trimmed beard and mustache, and short dark hair. He frowned at us as he closed the door, making sure it was locked behind him.

"We're closed," he growled.

"That's a shame," I said. I nodded at my car. "Got trouble with the exhaust. Think you could take a quick look at it?" Before he could bark back at me, I stopped him by taking out my license. "I know it's hard to see out here, but this is a private detective license. I was hoping you could help me. You Smitty, by any chance?"

"Ain't no Smitty," he said, squinting at the document in my wallet.

I'm sure he couldn't tell what the hell it was, but it made him feel like he was diligent. He nodded, and I put it away.

"Just the name of the place. I'm the owner, though. Brandon Lewis."

He stuck out his hand, and throwing caution to the wind, I shook it. He didn't crush my fingers, although I got the impression he'd have liked to, just to show his dominance. I noticed he had a backpack slung over his left shoulder and that he smelled slightly of Old Spice and cigarettes.

"How can I help you?" he asked, and then he looked down at Daisy, who was standing guard at my heels. "You always take your dog along on investigations? I'm assuming you're doing some sort of investigation."

"I am, and not always. The dog, I mean. As to what I'm investigating, I'm hoping you can tell me something about Graig Betz. I understand he works for you."

Lewis snorted. "Did. Hasn't shown up to work for days now. If you see him, tell him his ass is fired. I ain't got time for his bullshit."

"When was the last time you saw him?"

He looked up at the sky as he pondered the question. "Must have been, what, Wednesday? About three days ago, anyway. Yeah, he was supposed to be here at nine. Didn't show."

"How was his work up to that point? Did he often skip out for a day or so?"

Shaking his head, Lewis said, "No, up until then he was a good little worker. Always on time, never even called in sick."

"So what do you think happened to him? Is he the type to run off with some girl? Did he have a girl, do you know? Or a boy?"

Lewis's lip curled. "He weren't no fag. That's for sure. He had him a girlfriend, sure, but I don't think he ran off with her. She's been calling every day to see if I've heard from him, her and that grandmother of his. Wish they'd leave me alone. I ain't seen him."

I handed him one of my cards. "If you hear from him, or hear of someone who's seen him, give me a call." As he tucked the card into his pocket, I added, in an exaggerated imitation of his good-old-boy drawl, "Oh, and just for the record, I is one of them fags." And I curled my lip. So menacing.

Lewis stiffened, and I'm pretty sure his first instinct was to punch me in the face, but he thought better of it. Maybe he caught a glimpse of the holster under my jacket. His lips did a little dance of anger before he finally spat out some words. "I think I've told you all you need to know. Now if you'll excuse me, I've got a meeting to go to."

He made a point to shove against me as he walked to his car, and I'd be lying if I didn't say I nearly stumbled from what was probably to him just a gentle nudge. He got in his vehicle, a beat-up Chevy, but he was obviously waiting for Daisy and I to depart first, so we returned to our car.

"What do you say, a ride around the block a few times until we're sure he's gone, then we come back?"

Daisy didn't say anything, but I could tell she thought it was a splendid idea.

Because I knew she'd picked up on the same thing I had.

Several things, actually. When there was something supernatural around, I tended to know it. The little hairs on the back of my neck stood up and went, "Hey, dummy. Something is about to jump out and go boo!" It wasn't an infallible system, but when it kicked in, I took notice. And I was getting a trace of warning while I was amiably chatting with Brandon Lewis. It wasn't a full-on Klaxon, but it was there. Just enough to let me know he was up to something fishy.

Daisy was picking up on it too, unless her glare at him was because he had doggie treats in his pockets, which I seriously doubted. Plus, for her, doggie treats were squirrel brains, so doubly unlikely. She'd been watching him carefully, ready to chomp onto his leg if he made any false moves, like flicking my nose with his finger.

She also had a way of picking up on death. I didn't know if it was the smell of blood or if there was some cerebral connection since she was dead as well, but if someone had been offed recently, she knew. Her sniffer went into overdrive and she snorted and huffed and then looked up at me as if to wonder why I wasn't picking up on this stuff. And she did it during my interview with good old homophobic Brandon.

So I wanted a better look around Smitty's Autobody. Maybe I was wrong and Brandon was as sweet as honey, and I was just hoping to make him out as a baddie because of the way his lip twisted when he said "fags." On the other hand….

Daisy and I drove a few blocks away and then circled back. The parking lot was now empty and the place dark and closed up tight. I parked next door, at a bakery, just in case Brandon didn't trust me and circled back himself to make sure I'd gone for good. It would be just the sort of thing a sneaky bastard like him would do.

Daisy and I got out of the car and I let her lead the way. After all, she had the nose. I had a good flashlight with me, and my gun was handy and loaded with silver bullets. Oddly you couldn't get those at Kmart. I had to go to my other source, Gina. Not only did she make them herself, but she added a little mojo to them. How many high school teachers could boast they're also silversmiths?

We got back to the entrance, and Daisy was obviously picking up a scent. She did a few circles and then shot off around the side of the building. I followed. She kept on going to the alley behind the garage. I switched on my flashlight so I wouldn't trip over anything and tried my best to keep up with her.

She stopped in the alley near a dumpster. There was a dark stain in the dirt, and she pounced on it. You could almost hear her shout, "Eureka." Tail wagging, she looked up at me. I knelt down and examined the spot. Impossible to tell just by looking, especially as it was now nearly dry, but I'd bet the homestead (if I had one) we were looking at a bloodstain.

I stood after giving Daisy a congratulatory pat on the head. "So what are we thinking? If you're thinking that someone was gutted by a werewolf back here recently, I'd have to agree with you. And furthermore I'd say the body—" I paused to lift up the lid of the dumpster. "—is right in... this—" I looked inside. "—empty dumpster." I shrugged. "Well, it was worth a try."

Daisy was digging in the ground. All at once she stopped and looked up, ears alert.

"What is it, girl? What do you—?"

Then I heard it. A deep, guttural growl.

There was a streetlight at the end of the alley that threw enough light on the scene that I didn't really need the flashlight, so I switched it off. No reason to call attention to yourself when there was a nasty growly thing around. It was like saying, "Hey, come over here. I'm right behind this big old bright light." In seconds my gun was out of the holster and in my left hand.

The other end of the alley was now in deep shadow, and that's where the growling was coming from, and it was getting closer. Eventually I could see a shape. A big, hairy shape.

No, two big hairy shapes. Make that three.

Holy fucking shit. "Daisy," I said, backing up slowly, "how fast do you think you can run?"

I fired at the closest shape and got an angry yelp in return. The other two creatures scrambled to the side, uncertain now as to what they should do. One of them was now close enough to the light that I could get more details.

It was a wolf, but it wasn't a wolf. It was a man, but it wasn't a man. There were lots of different types of werewolves, from those who became the actual animal to dudes who just looked like they glued some hair onto their cheeks and used some putty on their noses. This was an amalgamation of man and wolf, maybe a little more on the wolf side. Big, covered in dark-gray fur, with a huge snout and very sharp-looking fangs. It was on all fours, but I could tell it was equally at home walking on two if need be.

And it didn't look happy.

I fired again, but it moved with incredible swiftness back into the shadows, snarling angrily. Maybe I nicked it; maybe I didn't. To be truthful I wasn't hanging around to find out. I was belting around the side of the building as fast as I could, Daisy beside me. I paused long enough to fire behind me, just to make sure they knew I still had bullets. I could hear them scrambling after us, but they were trying to keep in the shadows. I think they also were a little wary after I shot one of their comrades. Whatever caused their hesitation, I was grateful for it because Daisy and I made it to the car without being ripped to shreds. True, as Daisy hopped into the passenger seat, she had a complaining look that told me she thought we should be back there kicking werewolf butt, but I opted, for once, for caution.

As I started the engine, I muttered, "And this is me, running away."

Before I pulled out of the lot, though, I caught sight of one of the wolves, which was at the corner of Smitty's, watching us drive away. It was the biggest fucking werewolf I'd ever seen, standing erect, gripping the side of the building with one hairy paw. The damned thing had to be seven feet tall, maybe more. And it was packed with muscle. I had no doubt the wary eyes that were watching my car as I stomped on the gas belonged to none other than Brandon Lewis.

Something told me I shouldn't have handed him my business card.

CHAPTER 6

"BUT," NICK said, frowning over his gin and tonic, "there wasn't a full moon last night."

We were sitting at the main bar at the Slippery Noodle Inn, the oldest bar in town. Also one of the most popular, if the night's crowd was anything to go by. When I entered I chatted a little with the bouncer, whom I knew slightly. I was responsible for him doing time a couple of years back. Luckily he didn't seem to hold a grudge. I'd arranged to meet Nick there before his date with Casey to smooth over our ruffled feathers and to tell him about my experience the other night.

"Funny thing about werewolf legends," I said, moving my straw around just to annoy the ice cubes in my Captain Morgan and Coke. "Most of them were made up by Curt Siodmak, the writer of the movie *The Wolf Man.* And in that movie, Lon Chaney wolfs out whenever the wolfsbane blooms and the autumn moon is bright. The idea of a full moon happened in later pictures. I don't know if he thought he was making up the part where you can become a werewolf after being bit by one, but he got that right."

"So they can become wolves any time in the fall if the moon is out? I do need to point out that it's May."

"Fall, winter, spring, doesn't matter. Moon doesn't really matter either, for most types of lycanthropes. It can be a cloudy night, and they can transform."

"Lovely," Nick mumbled. "Remind me not to let my cats out at night anymore."

"You don't have to be bitten by a werewolf either, although that's the main way it works. Magic spells can achieve the same goal."

"So why aren't there werewolves everywhere?"

Nick was fidgeting. Either he didn't like the conversation or he was itching to see his new honey. Probably the latter.

"I mean, you get bit by one and—bam!—you're a werewolf!"

I tried some of my drink. Too much soda, not enough rum. To be fair, though, the bartender was tremendously busy with other customers. Nick was done with his gin, and every now and then he tried to catch the bartender's eye for a refill.

"Generally people don't survive a werewolf attack. They end up ripped to shreds. And along with vampires and other old-world-type ghoulies, they're a dying breed. Not too many of them left." Like witches. Gina was one of the last of her kind, although they were faring better than vamps and wolfies, mainly because they weren't, for the most part, vicious killers. "It's odd to find a pack in a city, though. Werewolves don't like crowds of people."

"So how many are there in this pack?" Nick finally got the bartender's eye and signaled for another drink.

I shrugged. "Not sure. Might be one less, though. I'm pretty sure I shot one."

Nick held off replying while he transacted business with the bartender. If the guy overheard us casually talking about werewolves, he might think we'd had one too many and cut us off. Once it was safe, Nick asked, "What if the one you shot was some poor guy who was bitten by a wolf? It's not really his fault. Isn't there some kind of cure? Couldn't Gina zap them or something?"

With a small smile, I told him, "Odd you should mention that. My silver bullets are made by Gina, and she gives them a little spell. If the wound isn't fatal, the bullet actually rids the person of the curse and he just ends up human again, although with a bullet hole in him. If the curse is due to magic, well, I've shot a werewolf."

"So the guy you shot might be okay."

I made a face, one of the sour variety. "Doubtful. If the bullet didn't kill him, his buddies probably did once he transformed back to human. I went back to the alley later, but there was no sign of carnage, so maybe it didn't hit him anyway. And Smitty's seems to have closed up shop permanently. They weren't open today at all, and calling only gives you their answering machine."

Nick gave me a hopeful smile. "So maybe you scared them."

"Yeah, they must have been shitting themselves with terror as Daisy and I were running away."

"They weren't expecting silver bullets, though."

"No, me being armed did seem to take them by surprise."

I realized I should have got another drink when Nick got his. My rum and Coke was gone, but now the bartender was down at the other end of the bar and busy as hell. Nick looked at his watch.

"I'm not keeping you from your date, am I?"

"No," he replied, "I've still got time."

There was an uncomfortable silence as I contemplated the scene at the restaurant, and I'm sure Nick was doing the same. "I really am sorry for outing you the other night," I finally said.

Nick made a you-can-be-a-dick-but-you're-my-friend-what-can-I-do face. "Eh," he said, "it's just weird that I pick a guy with psychic abilities to date."

"Maybe deep down you recognized that in each other. Who knows why one guy attracts us and another doesn't? Still, I was out of line. I should have let the two of you reveal your secrets on your own terms."

"So Casey can read your mind?"

"Sort of. We were having one hell of a conversation. That's for sure."

"He said he can't do that with too many people."

"Guess I'm just one of the lucky ones. But I really am sorry. I was just crabby that night, what with Robbie being gone and everything."

Nick shook his head. "About that. You're insisting he stay down there for a vacation that was supposed to be for the both of you, but it's obviously making you miserable. You can't stand to be away from him."

"True."

"So why not just tell him to come back?"

I took in a deep breath and let it out slowly. "You really want to know?"

"I asked, didn't I?"

The bartender wasn't responding to my obvious hint of holding a ten-dollar bill in my hand. "I'm terrified, to be honest."

"How so?" Nick asked with a frown.

The bartender saw me and motioned he'd be with me soon. Or maybe he was swatting away a fly. "For one thing, he's human now. Dead for over a decade, but now he's back, looking just the way he did when he died. He's got family that lives in town. It's a big city, but eventually one of them is going to spot him out somewhere. What's his mother going to think when she sees a walking, talking Robbie? One who hasn't aged a day since he died?"

Nick blinked. "Yeah, I can see that would be a worry."

"And then there's my work. He wants to help out, I know. He'd be devastated if I told him I didn't want him to come along with me, but…. Well, take the current case. Werewolves. I couldn't bear it if Robbie got hurt or killed. Especially killed. I don't ever want to go through that again."

I didn't think he could overhear us, but the guy on the stool on my right was getting one hell of a story to tell his friends if he could.

Nick reiterated. "A dead, ghost Robbie was okay to get involved in your cases, but an alive, human one is verboten."

"He can get hurt now."

"So can you."

"Yeah, but I'm an idiot. I'm used to this stuff."

"You didn't mind me coming along once in a while. I'm human."

"Actually I did. I was always worried about you. You just never took no for an answer."

Nick finished his second drink. I was way behind.

"You're going to have to talk to him. Tell him how you feel."

"Like that will work. He'd just come along anyway." The bartender brought me another drink. As I paid him, he gave me the briefest of smiles. Was it a flirty one? I couldn't tell. I turned to Nick. "I just know I can't lose him again."

"Then don't."

He made it sound so easy.

OUT IN the parking lot, I called Robbie before starting up the car. I'd parked near a telephone pole, and up on the wires were a line of birds. I didn't stop to count, but there were enough of them I thought of Alfred Hitchcock movies. One was a big crow. A really big crow. And it seemed to be watching me sitting there. I scowled at the bird, but it continued giving me the evil eye. I decided to ignore it.

"What have you been up to?" I asked as soon as Robbie answered his phone.

"Worked on my tan today."

He sounded happy, but it seemed forced. My guess was he was getting bored being on his own. It would take a lot of convincing to keep him down in Florida another couple of days. As for me, I missed him like crazy, but I didn't want him with me right now. My heart was torn, but it and my lower extremities were responding positively to the sound of his voice.

"Getting any sunburn?"

"Naw," he said. "I used sunscreen. Well, my nose is a little red and my shoulders are a tad burned, but otherwise I'm good. Browning up pretty good, if I do say so myself. I'm no longer pale as a ghost. Get it? Pale as a…. Geesh, tough crowd."

"I got it. It was funny."

"I could tell by your uproarious laughter. So how's the case you're working on?"

"Ended up being nothing. Now I'm working on a case involving a lost kitty. Nothing interesting."

"Ah, you won't tell me. Must be something fun, then. Spill it."

"Okay, it seems that there is a pack of werewolves. It's nothing."

"Let me check the flight schedule. I'll see how soon I can be back."

"Hold on a second, I—"

That's as far as I got. "Look," Robbie said, "I know you're worried about me. Hell, I'm worried about me. But I feel better if I'm with you, dangerous situations be damned. Someone's got to look out and make sure you don't end up as wolfie chow."

I sighed. Deeply. "Stay there for now. You've just got a couple of days left on the room rental, and I'm just doing the boring stuff right now. Looking. Searching. Asking questions. Well, and running." I told him about my fun evening at Smitty's Autobody.

"See?" he said when I finished the tale. "If I'd have been there, things would have gone differently."

"How?"

"I wouldn't just have run. I'd have screamed and run. Much more effective."

Chuckling, I said, "It's just that—"

"I know. You want me safe. News flash, Dunc. Our lives aren't safe. Besides, I've already died once. What are the odds of it happening again?"

Too good for my liking.

CHAPTER 7

AFTER LEAVING the bar, I once again drove by Smitty's. Still locked up tight as a drum. Undaunted, I decided to try some of Graig Betz's other hangouts. His grandmother provided me not only with some pictures of Graig, but also gave me a list of friends, acquaintances, and haunts. I decided to check on a girl Graig had been dating, at least up until his employment at Smitty's.

Maud told me Graig's girl, name of Laura Johnson, worked as a waitress at Pickin's. I knew Pickin's, as I'd been there on a case a while back, and unless they'd changed quite a lot in the intervening time, they didn't employ waitresses. The girls who worked at Pickin's were strippers, and the bartenders tended to be beefy guys who made sure you didn't touch the goods without forking over a lot of greenbacks. So Maud's darling little twenty-three-year-old grandson's girl was an ecdysiast. Pickin's usual patrons couldn't pronounce or spell ecdysiast, though, so the sign outside promised exotic dancers.

As it was a Monday, there wasn't a huge crowd, so parking wasn't a problem. It was also a little early for the place to really be jumping, which was good for me. The employees wouldn't be too busy to answer a few questions.

I started with the guy at the door who checked my ID (only a casual glance, the bastard!) and insisted I fork over a cover charge. Once we dispensed with the cash exchange, I showed him a picture of Graig Betz.

"Seen this guy lately?"

The door guy was big and muscular, with a shaved head. He probably thought he looked scary that way, but to me he resembled Curly from the Three Stooges. He eyed the photo briefly.

"Graig? Yeah, I know him. Comes in all the time. Why? He owe you money, bud?"

I shook my head. "Just looking for him. He been in lately?"

"Not for a week or so."

"Laura Johnson working tonight?" Master of the segue, that's me.

Curly frowned a moment before understanding dawned on him. "Oh, you mean Skylar! None of the girls used their real names here, naturally. Took me a moment to remember. Yeah, she's here." He glanced at a clock on the wall. "She won't be on until later tonight, though. You might find her at the bar."

I went in. I wasn't a fan of strip joints (couldn't imagine why!) in the first place, but there was something really sad about one on an off night. A few scattered drinkers ogling the dancers. The dancers seemed bored, knowing there weren't enough patrons for them to make much in the way of tips. The atmosphere was a mixture of desperation and sadness. One guy in particular was gazing up at a dancer with unbridled lust in his eyes. He seemed stinking drunk, and it was still early. I felt sorry for his liver.

At the main bar, which was away from the dancers, there were only a few souls sitting on the stools. One was a woman. She was probably in her early twenties, had blonde hair and pale, pale skin. Laura Johnson, better known as Skylar? If she was a stripper, she hadn't yet changed into her work outfit, although what she was wearing was sleazy enough. I took a chance and sat down next to her.

Beefy Bartender asked me what I wanted to drink. I was working, so I ordered a soda. If you wanted to be eyed like you just crawled out from under a rock, try being a dude and asking for a cola at a strip joint. Convinced I was insane, Beefy went off to get my drink. Once he was gone, I turned to the girl next to me.

"Laura Johnson, isn't it?"

Suspicion oozed from her blue eyes. "Do I know you?"

"No, but that's okay. A lot of people don't. My name is Duncan Andrews. I'm a private detective."

Her attitude thawed a fraction. "Yeah? What's that got to do with me?"

"I've been hired to find Graig Betz. Thought you might be able to help me out."

Laura seemed to melt on her bar stool, and she looked at me with a mixture of relief and hopefulness. "His grandmother hired you, didn't she?"

I nodded.

"Knew it. Couldn't have been anyone else. There's really no one else that cares about him, 'cept maybe an aunt somewhere. I don't think he has any other family left." She twirled on her stool so she was facing me. "Do you think you can find him? I've been trying, but he doesn't answer his phone, and—"

"I'll find him. Can you tell me about how he's been the last couple of weeks? Has he been acting strangely? Distant?"

Laura Johnson seemed glad to tell anyone, even a stranger, about Graig. A lot of it was similar to what Maud had observed. Graig became moody, especially after the sun went down. He disappeared often and wouldn't say where he'd been. Even his eating habits changed. Where once he liked his burgers and steaks well done, suddenly he would only eat meat if it was rare.

Maud reported to me she once spotted an animal outside of her house and could have sworn the wolflike creature then became her grandson. Moments later Graig knocked at her door, naked and wounded, asking for help. He didn't know his grandma saw him change before her eyes as she peered out her window, and he got angry when she asked for an explanation, saying he had a fight with his girlfriend and that was all anyone needed to know.

Laura hadn't seen Graig transform, but she did have a puzzling experience.

"He's been different in bed too," she said, the stories just pouring out of her. "Rough, you know? And before he was always so gentle. Kind and loving, if you know what I mean. And one night we were at my place and we were—"

She stopped suddenly, uncertain if she should be explicit with me.

"Fucking?" I supplied.

Laura Johnson smiled. "Yeah, and let me tell you, I wasn't enjoying it. He was like an animal. I still got a bruise on my hip! And I looked up at him, screaming for him to slow down, and… I don't know how to explain it. His eyes were red, almost glowing. It was just a second, but I swear it wasn't a reflection or anything. I think he was possessed or something."

I went through three sodas listening to Laura's stories, tipping the bartender liberally so he wouldn't think me a philistine. Now my bladder was yearning to be emptied, so I decided I'd heard almost enough from Laura. I hoped she could fill me in a little more, though. "And all this happened since he started working for Smitty's?"

Laura nodded.

I touched her hand. She looked like she needed comforting. "I'll do what I can to help Graig. Promise. One more thing and then I'll leave you alone. Do you know where Brandon Lewis lives?"

Bingo. She did.

"YOU NEED an army. You know that, don't you?"

It was the next day and Gina and I were doing a drive-by, checking out Brandon's crib. We hadn't found the actual house yet, but judging by the neighborhood I wasn't expecting something out of *Better Homes and Gardens.*

"Got one," I said, turning onto a street where the houses looked even more disreputable than the ones we had already passed. The crack houses in this area probably moved so they could get a better clientele. "You, me, Elton. He owes me a favor, what with me avenging the death of his rat."

Gina glanced at the passenger side door. I'm pretty sure she was checking to make sure it was locked. "News flash, Duncan. I'm not going in to fight a pack of werewolves. They tend not to sit still while I recite an incantation, and I have no intention of being ripped to shreds."

"You'd hang back, of course. Give me and Elton a protection spell, that sort of thing."

She shook her head. "They're too strong and too fast. Even with a protection spell, you and Elton can't handle a pack all on your own."

"I was thinking about asking Ted Nugent to join us. I hear he likes shooting things."

Gina was watching a cat that was on somebody's porch. The cat watched the car go by, or maybe it was keeping an eye on Gina. Witches and cats. Someday I'd have to ask her about the connection. "How about Robbie?" she asked. "You've been giving him lessons."

"Shooting beer cans and shooting werewolves are two totally different things."

"In other words this is too dangerous for him."

"Damn right."

"Isn't that for him to decide?" She was looking at me now and smiling gently.

"Nope," I said.

"Well, that's fair." She patted my knee. "You lead a dangerous life. You can't protect him all the time, you know."

"Watch me try."

"Having him with you might be a good thing," she said. "You tend to be a little reckless. With Robbie by your side, you might be more careful. Save me from having to heal your wounds all the time."

"Worrying about him would slow me down."

I was creeping along but slowed even more as we got close to the house in question. It looked abandoned. The grass was high, at least where there was grass, and the building itself looked like a slight breeze could knock it over. The porch was sagging, tiles were missing from the roof, and at least two windows were boarded up. A two-story house, it looked like it hadn't seen a fresh coat of paint in my lifetime. There was a gravel driveway and a decrepit garage with a broken main door. There was no movement anywhere.

"Sure she gave you the right address?" Gina asked.

The hairs on the back of my neck were bristling. "Yeah. This is it. He's either asleep or not home. No car in the drive, so I'm guessing he's out." Lewis certainly wasn't at work. Smitty's Autobody was still closed.

"So what's your plan?"

I sped up, having seen what I needed to see. "You said I needed an army. I don't. The plan is to get Lewis on his own, with no pack to back him up. If he wolfs out, I'll shoot him with my trusty gun. If he remains in human form, I'll try to reason with him."

"Did he seem like the reasonable type?"

I didn't have to think about that for long. "No. So I'll hope he wolfs out and I'll shoot him. His pack will be disoriented then, and I'll be able to easily find them and dispose of them accordingly."

"You'll try to wound them first, and cure them."

"Yep."

"What if they don't want to be cured?"

"I'm not going to give them the option." A few turns and we were back in at least a semidecent neighborhood. "Or course, I've got to wait for them to wolf out. Can't shoot them in human form. The bleeding gets so messy."

"That and your rule against shooting humans unless absolutely necessary."

"Yeah, that too."

Ahead was a sign we'd returned to civilization. A McDonald's. Opposite it was a supermarket that seemed fairly busy. People buying carrots and cheese and Greek yogurt, totally unaware a werewolf lived less than a mile away.

"THANKS FOR seeing me," Casey said.

"Well," I said, hoping I looked as contrite as I felt, "it's the least I could do. Besides, I wanted to apologize in person for the other day."

We were at an Olive Garden near the Applebee's we ate at the other night. I ordered spaghetti because it was that kind of a night and I didn't mind if I spattered my shirt with tomato sauce. Casey asked for lasagna. We were sipping wine while waiting for our food. So far I hadn't heard any of his thoughts. Apparently he had shut off his ability for the time being.

"No need," he said. "Besides, it all had to come out at one time or another. Nick and I have it all sorted out now."

"That's good." I didn't think I was hungry, but I found myself wishing the waiter would come with my spaghetti. The salad was good, but I wanted something I could slurp, and Robbie still wasn't around.

Casey looked around the dining room. "So. Any ghosts in here?"

I shook my head. "Relatively unhaunted. Or maybe they're just off resting. Either way I haven't spotted any."

"Have you always had the ability to see ghosts?"

"Born that way. Got it from my dad. My mother thought we were nuts. Actually she still thinks I'm nuts. My dad died years ago. How about you?"

He swallowed some salad before he spoke, leaving just a drop of dressing on his chin. "Same, although my mother had the shining, not my dad. I got it from her."

"Do you get premonitions, like the kid in the Stephen King book?"

Casey made a face, and I couldn't tell if he was pondering the question or if some of the salad went down the wrong way.

"Sometimes. But nothing really detailed. I really just get vague impressions. Getting one now, in fact."

"From me?"

He nodded. "I don't know how much you should put into this, considering your job, but I'm getting the vibe that you're in danger. Big danger. Whatever you're involved in, be careful."

"Always," I said, lying through my teeth.

Conversation halted with the arrival of our main courses. Casey waited until the waiter was gone and we had a few bites before continuing.

"Nick's told me all about you."

"And you still asked me out for dinner?"

He smiled gently and blew on a forkful of lasagna. "He still has strong feelings for you, you know."

"I thought you couldn't read his mind?"

"I can't, but I can see how he looks at you and read his body language. Oh, I don't think he's still got a flame in his heart burning for you. He did at one time, but now it's more wondering what things would have been like under different circumstances." He shoveled the pasta into his mouth and chewed carefully. "I know about Robbie."

"All of it?"

Casey nodded. "That's gotta be… weird."

"That's one word for it. I prefer to concentrate on the positives, like the sex."

He frowned as he picked up his wineglass. "But you're also afraid. Terrified, in fact. Of losing him again."

I had been twirling spaghetti around my fork. Only two spots on my shirt so far. I paused to look up at Casey. "I thought you weren't reading my mind right now."

"I didn't have to. It's all in your eyes. Your love for him and the worry."

I've got to start wearing dark glasses around Casey. "We'll work it out," I said.

"Do you want my advice?"

"I find that people who say that tend to give it no matter the response."

Casey smiled. "Then here it is. Robbie is your life. And that I did get from being in your mind the other day. So don't try to cut him out of part of it. It won't work. You two are connected in a very strong way. Deep down you know that. You're a better person when he's with you."

"Thanks. I think."

So stop torturing yourself. Casey's voice was in my head again.

I concentrated. *Advice taken and accepted.*

We ate the rest of the meal in silence, although we did talk a lot.

CHAPTER 8

I LOOKED at my cell phone for the tenth time to check the time. Where was Robbie? His flight landed fifteen minutes ago. Surely he'd gathered up his baggage by now.

My car and I were waiting, against the rules, by the curb outside the Delta gate. My gaze alternated from the big sliding glass doors to see if Robbie was emerging to the rearview mirror to check if airport security was going to ask me to move along. They had what they called a cell phone lot, where you could park for free and wait for the passenger to call and tell you he had his bags and was waiting at the curb to be picked up, but I wanted to see Robbie without delay.

Nearby a whistle was being blown. I twisted around and saw a security guard waving at my car, shouting that I couldn't park there. I signaled I'd just be a moment by holding up one finger. He shouted something else. I contemplated switching fingers, but then I saw a familiar figure out of the corner of my eye. Robbie had just come out of the terminal.

I say familiar, but yet he wasn't. He was tanned, for one thing, with a peeling nose and very red forehead. Robbie was wearing a blue tank top, shorts, sandals, and a huge grin. He also had something on his cheeks and chin, and I thought for a moment that he'd been playing in the mud or just eaten some chocolate ice cream that decided to attack him instead. A closer inspection revealed, however, he was now sporting facial hair. Sort of.

I got out of the car and was in his arms before the security guard had time to blow his whistle again.

I still hadn't gotten used to how good he felt, the wonder of feeling him next to me. And his scent, a mixture of Dial soap, shampoo, and sweat. I'd never tell him, but every night we were apart I slept on his pillow, just to fall asleep breathing in the remembrance of him. Yes, having him alive after over ten years was causing some problems, but they were solvable ones, and I'd face any obstacle to keep him alive and well.

Even with the facial scruff.

Robbie was hugging me so tight it hurt, although it was a good hurt. To get him to ease up, I kissed his sunburned forehead. Still grinning, he raised his face to kiss me. Somewhere behind us the security guard was having a conniption fit and was in danger of wearing out his whistle. I gave him a mental finger, as I couldn't be bothered to release my grip on Robbie, at least not for the foreseeable future.

Eventually Robbie pulled his face away. "I think someone's trying to get our attention."

"You think?" Reluctantly I broke off the hug and leaned over to grab his bag. "Let's get out of here before I shove that whistle so far up that guy's ass a dentist will have to remove it."

As I was tossing Robbie's suitcase into the trunk, he stood close to me, beaming.

"So what do you think?"

"About what?" I asked, feigning innocence.

He rubbed his cheeks and chin. "The beard and mustache."

"Is that what you're calling it?"

"What?" He continued to finger the tufts of fur. "It's only a few days' growth. You've got to give it time."

We moved to get into the car, and the security guard turned his attention to another parking bastard. I buckled my seat belt and said, "Honey, I hate to break this to you, but… it's pretty… well, patchy."

Robbie curled his lip slightly with disappointment. "Yeah, my brain thinks I'm in my thirties, but my body insists it's twenty. And the body's winning."

I pulled away from the curb and reached over to jostle him playfully. "I'm teasing. You look beautiful. You couldn't look anything but beautiful. Even if you do have yak hair glued onto your cheeks."

He chuckled. "I thought it would help. A sort of disguise, you know. And I can wear these." He had a pair of sunglasses attached to the top of his tank top. He put these on and turned to beam at me proudly.

I did a double take as I navigated through the impossible traffic surrounding the airport.

"You look like you're auditioning for a reboot of the *Men in Black* movies."

"Or *Terminator*," he said, switching to an Arnold imitation. "I'll be back!" Smiling gently, he took off the shades. "I'll shave when we get home."

"Well," I said with a shrug, "not right away. First we have to close Daisy out of the bedroom and do nasty things to each other. One, it's been days since we've made love, and two, I want to see what it's like fucking an unshaven Robbie."

"I imagine it'll be much the same, just with the added danger of bristle burn."

Now that he was with me, I was mentally kicking my own backside. Nick was right. Robbie's place was by my side. How in the hell did I think him staying down in Florida without me was a good idea?

Although he did look happy, and the poor guy hadn't been away from Indianapolis for ages. We'd just have to make up for lost time.

I was about to utter an apology when my cell phone rang. I had placed it on the console between us. "Answer that, will you?" I said. There were too many cops around, and besides, being a responsible citizen—yeah, right!—I never used a cell phone while driving. Almost never.

Robbie scooped it up and answered with, "Andrews Detective Agency. Spooks our specialty. What can I do ya for?"

I chuckled even as I wanted to smack him.

"I'm his secretary," he went on to say. "Can I take a message for him?" His face grew grave as he listened. "I'll let him know. I'm sure he'll be right there, ma'am. Stay put and try not to worry."

I didn't like the seriousness of his tone. "What is it?"

He turned to me, a little pale under his tan. "That was a Mrs. Betz. Seems someone delivered a severed finger to her door this morning."

"It CAME all wrapped up like a Christmas present," Maud said. "I saved the wrapping, just in case you needed to see it."

The police certainly would. For now, though, I just looked at the box sitting on the coffee table in Maud's small but tastefully sweet apartment. It was the sort of box expensive gift pens came in. I lifted the lid slowly, having first put on a pair of latex gloves. No reason to get more prints on the thing than necessary. Surely enough, nestled in tissue paper, there was a severed human finger.

It didn't belong to Graig, not unless he'd done a Michael Jackson and became white. The digit was someone's pinkie finger, short and stubby. I couldn't tell for sure, but it looked like it had been bitten off. I closed the lid and took off the gloves.

"There was this note attached to it," Maud said as she laid a piece of paper down next to the box.

It was about four inches wide and seven inches long, probably torn from a notepad. On it was scrawled the words "Should have kept your mouth shut, Grandma."

"How did you find it?" I asked. "What time?"

Mrs. Betz looked very tired and more sad than disgusted with her find. "About ten o'clock. There was a knock at the door. I thought it was odd since I wasn't expecting anyone. I even hoped that it might be Graig. There was no one there when I opened the door, though. Just this box laying there."

"Neighbors see anything?" Robbie asked.

We were sitting on the couch, the evidence facing us on the table. Mrs. Betz was opposite us in an armchair that looked dainty and grandmotherly. It suited her. She eyed Robbie as if truly noticing him for the first time. In her defense she had had quite a shock.

"I don't know. I haven't talked to them."

She shot me a questioning look as if to check to see if he was qualified to ask questions of her.

I was so concerned with seeing the finger I hadn't bothered with introductions when we arrived. I rectified the situation by saying, "This is Robert Church. Robbie to his friends. Robbie, this is Maud Betz."

"Pleased to meet you, Robbie," Maud said. "Are you the secretary?"

Robbie was about to answer, but I stopped him. "He's my partner." In more ways than one.

He glanced at me briefly and tried to hide the pleasure my words gave him. He sat up and attempted a dignified pose, which was hard to do when you were wearing a tank top and shorts.

"A neighbor might have spotted the messenger, or at least someone acting suspiciously. We'll have to check."

"It's not your grandson's finger," I noted unnecessarily.

Mrs. Betz shook her head. "It's not Graig's handwriting either. There's no way he wrote this note. Dear Lord, some poor person has been mutilated, just as a warning to me. I feel so...."

She didn't have the words to describe her feelings, but she didn't need them. Her face said it all. I leaned forward. "This wasn't for you. It was for me. They know I'm looking for your grandson, and they're not happy about it. This was to get you to call off the case."

Maud's jaw was set. "Then they've underestimated me."

I smiled encouragingly at her. "Me too."

WE CALLED Lieutenant Carson, and he arrived in pretty good time. While we waited, Robbie checked on a few of the neighbors, but no one saw who left the package. We told Carson the basics, leaving out the werewolf bits. As far as he knew, we were hired to find Mrs. Betz's grandson, who was hanging out with some undesirable friends, and she was sent the finger as retribution and a warning. I also didn't mention my good buddy Brandon Lewis, not wanting Carson to go blundering in and get in over his head. Let's face it; he and his men just weren't equipped to deal with a pack of werewolves. Hell, I wasn't sure I was.

My admiration for Maud soared as she answered Carson's questions and she followed my lead. Even when pressed she revealed nothing to Carson we hadn't already covered. I could tell Carson knew something fishy was going on, but he knew when he was licked. He and his men left with the note and the box containing the finger, now in evidence bags, but not before taking me aside and telling me he'd want to know what was really going on and we'd have to talk later. I assured him we would.

Once Robbie and I were dismissed, we headed on to our apartment. Robbie sat in the passenger seat, beaming.

"So," he said. "Does this mean I'm on the payroll?"

"Yeah," I said, going along with the joke. "You'll get your check on Friday."

"Does this come with benefits? Health? 401K?"

"Considering that you don't officially exist, having died years ago, that might present difficulties."

Robbie became serious again. "Whose finger do you think it is?"

"Some homeless guy would be my guess. Maybe just some poor slob who was in the wrong place at the wrong time. We may never know."

"And the rest of him?"

"The bits that weren't devoured are probably in the White River."

Making a sour face, Robbie said, "We're having pasta for dinner tonight. I'm off meat for a few days."

"Fine by me." Actually my stomach would have appreciated any additions to its contents, as I missed lunch due to picking up Robbie and then dealing with cut-off fingers, not to mention Carson and his crew.

I didn't actually speed on our way to our apartment, but I didn't tarry either. As I parked in front of our building, I tried to think of what was in the refrigerator. Not much, I recollected. We got out of the car, and I was about to suggest hitting a restaurant after taking Daisy out when I got that tingly feeling Robbie called my Spidey sense. It was faint but there.

"We've had visitors," I said.

Robbie knew enough to trust my instincts. "Shit," he said. "In broad daylight?"

He had a point. If it were Brandon Lewis in human form, my alarm system wouldn't have kicked in. Only paranormal creatures made the hairs on the back of my neck bristle. Did Lewis or one of his cronies actually transform and pay us a visit?

If so they certainly won points by being bold.

I didn't feel they were still around, which was a good thing, as I'd left my gun at home. They frowned on firearms at the airport, strangely enough. Robbie and I rushed inside, although I made sure I was slightly ahead of him.

There was no way Lewis or anyone else could have gained entry to the apartment. Gina had so many spells protecting the premises that almost nothing could enter without my approval, ghosts excepted. Magic didn't work very well on those from the spirit world. I was concerned, though, about our neighbors. Finding they couldn't get into my pad, Lewis (or whomever) might have decided to take out their frustrations elsewhere.

Inside we found our door had received a little damage. There was a big swipe of a claw mark marring the surface and more scrapes and scratches around the doorknob.

We stood for a moment, just staring at the mutilated door. Finally Robbie shrugged and said, "I think you must have done something to annoy them."

CHAPTER 9

"IT HAD to have been a dog," our neighbor, Mrs. Russell, said.

She lived across the hall from us and was about my age, although she seemed older. Maybe it was the way she kept her hair tightly coiled in a series of buns. Despite the building rules, she was smoking a cigarette as she stood watching as I taped some cardboard over the claw marks. It would have to do until the door could be repaired, and I didn't want everyone in the building coming to gawk at the damage. The neighbors would think I had weird people who came to visit me.

Robbie was out with Daisy. We still hadn't eaten, so I was slightly cranky, and I raised an eyebrow at Mrs. Russell. "Um… this high on the door?"

She wasn't fazed. "It jumped."

Let her think it was a dog. "Did you see anything?" I asked, knowing full well Mrs. Russell often kept watch at her peephole, just to see who came to call at the Andrews residence. In her defense it probably was fairly entertaining.

"Well, I don't spy on my neighbors, of course…."

"No. Of course not."

"But I did hear a ruckus out here in the hall. Someone was banging and hollering, making a right old fuss. It sounded like they were trying to break your door down!"

Mrs. Russell took a drag off her nearly finished cigarette and blew the smoke in my face.

"Naturally I was concerned! I looked out the peephole, my phone in my hand, ready to call the police. Just as I got there, though, whoever it was ran off. I just got a glimpse of their dog as it ran after them. Big thing it was. Must have been a mastiff or something."

"Or something," I muttered.

She let out a bark of a laugh and smacked me on the shoulder. "At first I thought it was a bear! Granted, it was gone in a flash, but it almost seemed like it was walking on its hind legs. It's hard to really see things clearly through those peepholes, you know."

I stepped back to examine my handiwork. It looked stupid but better than a clawed door. I was barely paying attention to Mrs. Russell now. From her account, it seemed that one of the wolfies came to call and, when they found they couldn't break in, got a little miffed and did the only thing they could—scrape my door. No one spotted a human transforming into a beast, and no one got hurt, although Daisy was in a fighting mood when we finally entered the apartment. Seemed zombie bulldogs didn't care much for werewolves. Go figure.

"Couldn't have been a bear, though, could it?" I said once Mrs. Russell's words sank in.

She went to take another puff, only to find there wasn't enough left. I thought she was going to drop the cig and grind it under her fluffy pink mule, but she refrained.

"One could have escaped from the zoo."

"And what would it have been doing here? Trying to sell me Avon products?"

"Well, something made that mark on your door, and you can bet the management's not going to be happy. The whole thing will have to be replaced!"

The grooves left in the door were pretty deep, so she was probably right. My only solace was that the creature must have gotten one hell of a jolt from the protection spells as his claws marred my door.

Still, this meant the pack knew where I lived, which wasn't good. It also meant we'd all have to be on our toes until the problem of Brandon Lewis was solved once and for all. Despite the chance of someone catching sight of Daisy munching on the brains of her squirrel prey, I insisted Robbie take her to a park that was well populated. I'd rather have someone throw up seeing a squirrel being ravaged by a dead bulldog than take a chance on Robbie running into Lewis or one of his gang without a lot of witnesses handy.

Assuming they were smart enough not to morph in front of a crowd. Maybe I was giving them too much credit.

Either way, Lewis and company were quickly becoming a thorn in my side.

ROBBIE, GINA, Elton, and I were having a planning meeting. Robbie had been doing some research and had his notes handy. He'd also shaved the scuff off his face, thankfully. We were gathered around my dining room table, which was littered with paper plates and now-empty pizza cartons. I thought six pizzas would be enough, but the rest of us had to eat quickly to keep Elton from scarfing down the lot. I didn't know if demons in general favored pizza, but Elton certainly did, although, as a newly vegetarian demon, he preferred plain old cheese. I noticed, though, once all the plain slices were gone, he helped himself to some sausage and pepperoni. Still, he was trying.

Daisy was off in the corner, sleeping and digesting her evening meal.

"My guess is that they don't spend much time in the city, not in wolf form, anyway." Robbie made a sour face as he sipped his wine. Sodas were more his style, but we were out. "There haven't been reports of weird creatures running around the streets at night. So either they're really, really careful—and werewolves aren't famous for being circumspect—or they're taking their lycanthroping out to the country."

Elton burped, muttered an apology, and then nodded. "Makes sense. The city isn't exactly a good spot for wolves to roam."

"Plus," Robbie added, consulting his notes, "we've got reports of cattle mutilation around Lebanon and even as far north as Lafayette. A couple of teenagers from Clarks Hill were out parking one night, and they swear they saw, and I quote, 'Several big animals, sort of like wolves but much scarier.' They thought they'd found a colony of Sasquatches. The local sheriff's department didn't put a lot of stock into the claim, as the kids were pretty inebriated."

"People don't still believe in Sasquatch, do they?" scoffed Elton. I could tell he was wanting to light up one of his cigarettes, but we were strictly a nonsmoking household.

"Said the guy with yellow skin and horns growing out of the top of his head."

Robbie and Elton hadn't spent a lot of time together, but they'd already formed a pretty good friendship. They liked to needle each other. Elton's nickname for Robbie was "the now living one." Jokingly he'd often lick his lips as he eyed Robbie and rub his stomach as if he was hungry and Robbie was a tasty morsel. At least I hope he was doing it jokingly.

"The question is," Gina interjected, "are all of the pack werewolves because they want to be? Or were they bitten?"

I nodded. "If they're werewolves against their will, we have to get them to Gina. She can cure them."

"Can't we just kill them?" Elton asked. "I'm not trying to be difficult here, but if they're in wolf form, they're not exactly going to listen to reason. You can't sit them down and say, 'Is this really what you want to do?' That's difficult when they're trying to rip your throat out."

"We kill only when we have to," I said. "We're going under the assumption that the pack leader, Brandon Lewis, is a werewolf by design. We don't know for sure about the others. And either way, I'd like to get Graig Betz back in one piece for his grandmother's sake."

"Since they've already targeted this apartment," Gina added, "we have to assume that none of us are safe. I've made charms for all of us. Wear them at all times. Unfortunately I can't tell how effective they are until we put them to the test. So don't go into a scuffle with them thinking you're invincible."

For some reason she glared at me during the last sentence.

She passed the necklaces around. They had pentagrams on them.

Elton held his up against his chest gingerly, as if afraid it would burn through his Brooks Brothers shirt. "A pentagram? Isn't that rather predictable?"

Gina smiled at him. "I could have made them little ducky symbols. It's the charm that matters, not the emblems themselves."

"We also don't go outside," I said, "unless we're armed. Guns with silver bullets, and everyone gets a silver dagger, which you can strap to your leg." I slid a brand-new shiny .357 revolver across the table to Robbie. "That will stop anything coming your way."

He tapped it with his pencil first, then picked it up to get a better look. "I should hope so," he said. "Is it loaded?"

"Not yet. The nice thing about a .357 is that .38 rounds will work as well, so if you run out of bullets, you can always borrow some of mine. Of course, for the time being, we'll be using ammunition supplied by Gina. It's got added oomph."

"He got me a Walther P22," Gina said. "It looks like something out of *The Terminator.*" She leaned seductively toward me. "You always get me the loveliest gifts."

I went on, ignoring the fact Gina was thrusting her breasts at me. "Silver ain't cheap, so try to make every shot count. Wound if at all possible. We'll hit the firing range tomorrow at Don's Guns so that everyone can get comfortable with firing their weapons."

Elton did his best to look affronted. "And I get jack shit?"

"Well, I thought… it might be insulting to offer a demon something so mundane as a gun."

His lips widened into a wicked grin. "That's okay. I've got these." He held up his hands, making sure the talons were extended.

"Of course you don't have to help out with this at all."

Elton shrugged. "It's the least I could do, what with you helping me avenge Herman."

I could be wrong, but I think his eyes got a little misty at the mention of his dead rat's name.

Robbie was still checking out his Smith and Wesson. "Am I licensed for this?"

I made an "eh" face. "Sort of. I'd prefer it if you didn't get picked up by the police while carrying your little cannon. Your IDs are good, but I'd hate for them to be held up to too much scrutiny." Ah, the difficulties of being alive after you've been dead for years.

"And Nick?" Gina asked.

"I've told him to be careful, especially at night. I doubt if he's in any danger since he hasn't been around here much since he started dating

Casey. The pack probably doesn't know about him. He volunteered to help out, but I told him to stay put on this one. Too dangerous."

Elton grunted. "Not too dangerous for us, though, I notice."

"You're a big nasty-clawed demon. Gina can take care of herself, and Robbie—"

He looked up from his gun expectantly. There was just a hint of worry in his eyes, and I'm sure he thought I was going to say he'd have to stay at home most of the time.

"—his place is by my side. We'll do the best we can." I smiled. I knew how to encourage the troops.

"Now," Gina said, slapping the table, "we just have to find the bastards."

Robbie's eyes strayed over to the door. "If they don't find us first."

CHAPTER 10

I WAS dreaming of puppies when the phone rang.

Actually I couldn't tell you what I was dreaming about, but I knew I didn't want to have it interrupted. With my eyes still bleary, I raised my head just enough so that I could see the clock on my nightstand. It was just after seven in the morning.

Next to me Robbie stirred briefly under the covers and said something that sounded like "Wazz a bant hall mart?" I have no idea what he was trying to convey, but I agreed with him wholeheartedly.

Guessing he was asking who was disturbing his slumbers, I said, "I don't know. I'll find out."

The phone in the bedroom was an actual telephone, cord and everything. Our home phone was a private number, and only a few people had it. I assumed it would be Gina, as she was the most likely candidate, but when I answered, I heard Elton's deep growl. I only gave our friendly—well, sort of friendly—demon the number a few days previously.

"They were busy last night" was his opening line. No "hello, how are you." Demons had no sense of etiquette.

I sat up and rubbed my face, trying to get my brain to function properly. "The Kardashians?"

My quip got a grunt. Demons weren't hot on humor either. To be fair, though, Elton was a laugh riot compared to most.

"Our lycanthropes."

I rolled my neck to get a kink out and was rewarded with a lovely little crack. Robbie's eyes were open now, and he was up on his elbows, eyeing me with heavy lids.

"Who is it?" he asked.

I mouthed "Elton" at him and then said into the phone, "What happened?"

"Whole family was killed last night. Four people. I heard it on the radio. They aren't giving many details, but apparently it was pretty brutal."

"What makes you think our buddies were involved?"

"A friend of mine tipped me off."

Elton wasn't a typical demon, considering he strove to be human, but he continued to keep in touch with some of his old cronies. "Did this friend see anything?"

"He was nearby and heard the screams. He said that when he checked it out, he saw some werewolves leaving the house by the back windows. Two of them, maybe three. He wasn't sure."

"Shit." I slid my legs over the side of the bed and cradled the phone against my shoulder so I could grab a pen and a notepad. "Do you have the address?"

Elton did. It was a place on the west side of town, not far from the Indianapolis Speedway. I thanked Elton for the information.

He grunted again. "Don't mention it. We get to kill them soon, don't we?"

"Very," I replied as I hung up.

IT WASN'T easy getting in contact with Lieutenant Dave Carson. Everyone I spoke to told me they'd be glad to take a message and relay it to him, but for some reason, I was reluctant to tell the police department I thought the house on Bertrand Road was attacked by werewolves. Finally I just told someone to tell him I might have some information about the killings. That got through, as he called me within two minutes.

The first words out of his mouth were "You know, I should have known this would have something to do with you." Police and demons sometimes had the same manners.

"And good morning to you too, Lieutenant," I said. We were still in the bedroom, but I was dressed now, and Robbie was nearly there. He was cussing as he buttoned up his shirt, as he was hurrying and his fingers were fumbling the job.

"Is this one of your weird killers?" Carson barked at me. "Some kind of... hell, I don't know. What is it we're dealing with here?"

"Do you really want to talk about it over the phone?" I asked.

Carson agreed with me. Well, to be accurate, he let out a string of cuss words, some of which I was sure he invented. Then he growled, "How soon can you get here?"

"Half an hour."

Carson gave me the address. I didn't have the heart to tell him I already had it and that I received the info from a demon. I said a cheery farewell. Carson muttered a few more curse words.

I hung up and turned to see Robbie standing by the closet, shrugging into a dark-blue suit jacket. Something in my face must have alarmed him because he examined his attire in panic.

"What? Am I covered in lint or something? What?"

The truth was the only time I'd seen him in a suit was at his funeral, and the memory wasn't a pleasant one. I dredged up a smile. "Nothing. You look fine."

He grinned. "I thought that now that I was a partner, I ought to dress for the occasion. This is okay without a tie, isn't it? People don't wear ties much anymore, not for everyday. It's more just a wedding thing now."

And funeral.

I sighed and shook my head to dispel the mood I was putting myself into. Robbie was alive now, and thinking about that horrible time was a waste of energy. Still, that hollow feeling I had in my heart when he died would always be a part of me.

"You look good," I said. It was the truth. "Where did you get the suit?"

"Bought it a few days ago. I went out shopping with Gina. I was going to surprise you with it and wear it for your birthday, but now I guess I'll have to think of something else." He leered at me, and as he walked by me, he pinched my butt. "You coming?" he asked.

It wasn't hard to locate the right house, as patrol cars were parked along the street and officers were stationed to keep gawkers from getting too close. The uniformed cop who stopped us peered hard at my license before letting us past the barricade. Robbie and I strode up the walk side by side, me with maybe just a tad more swagger. Robbie pointed at a crow that was perched on the roof.

"That is one ginormous crow," he said.

It was indeed. "They seem to be getting big nowadays."

There was another officer at the door, apparently keeping track of who came and went. I recognized him, and he smiled grimly as I approached.

"Duncan Andrews," he said. "People get ripped to shreds, so of course you're on the scene."

"Ah, Officer Moore, it's good to see you too."

He motioned with his thumb. "Carson's waiting for you inside. Try not to step in the blood."

He wasn't joking. My first impression as I stepped over the threshold was I'd just entered a slaughterhouse. The front door led directly into the living room, and it was a mess, with blood on the carpets, blood on the walls, and even blood spatters on the ceiling. There wasn't any sign of bodies—or parts—so I assumed they'd already been carted away. There were a few cops and plainclothes guys loitering around, chatting and taking notes and generally grumbling. Some had coffee cups in their hands that looked like they'd come from a nearby gas station. Everyone looked tired and anxious to leave the place.

In the middle of the room was Lieutenant Carson, chatting with another plainclothes dude. Carson was unshaven and looked more rumpled than Columbo. When he spotted me, he raised a finger to tell me he'd be with me in a minute. Or maybe he raised the wrong finger.

Robbie was gazing about the room in awe. "Holy crap. They really went to town in here."

"Looks like it."

Carson finished his chat and came over to us. He didn't seem in a good mood. "Who's this?" he asked, pointing at Robbie.

"This is my partner, Robert Davis," I said, using the name we put on his fake ID. Legally, Robbie Church was dead and buried years ago. Resurrections come with their own sets of problems. "Rob, this is the infamous David Carson of the Indianapolis Metropolitan Police Department."

Scowling, Carson raised his coffee cup to his lips without drinking. "You look awfully young," he told Robbie. "You do realize you're working for a nut, don't you?"

"I've kind of figured that out," Robbie said with a nod.

"Yeah, well, hopefully he won't get you killed." Carson took a sip and winced. "Damn stuff is cold. So you know something about this?" The last bit was directed at me.

"Possibly."

He glanced around to make sure we couldn't be overheard. "Does it have anything to do with the old woman and the severed finger?"

"In a roundabout way."

"And is it paranormal in nature?"

"Definitely."

Carson rolled his eyes skyward as if asking for help. He then closed them. "Tell me again why I don't run you out of town."

"Because then you'd have to deal with this kind of shit yourself. And believe me, you don't want to."

He glanced around and saw we were in close proximity to several of his men. "Let me take you into the master bedroom. There's no one in there right now, and we can talk."

A short trip down the hall brought us to the room in question. This room had been the scene of tragedy as well. The rumpled sheets on the bed were soaked in drying blood, and there were splashes on the walls. A uniformed cop followed us and asked Carson if he needed anything. Carson told him a vacation and then sent the guy on his way. Once the three of us were alone, Carson rubbed a weary hand through his thinning hair.

"First off, how did you find out about this? We haven't released any details yet."

"Connections," I said. It was better if he didn't know that connection was a demon. "But honestly we really don't know what happened here, although I have one hell of a working theory."

"We got an anonymous tip shortly after midnight. I was at home, sleeping the sleep of the just. I got here about one o'clock. Far as we can tell, there were three family members slaughtered, ripped to shreds. We haven't determined just how yet. The ME said it looked to him like an animal attack, but I can't figure out how that would be possible. Maybe you can enlighten me."

"Probably. Who were the victims?"

"Father, Sheldon Elliot. Forty-three years of age. Worked for Eli Lilly. He was found there," Carson said, nodding at the bed, "with his lovely wife Allison. Allison had multiple lacerations across her throat and chest. Looks like she bled to death. Mr. Elliot received wounds to the neck and chest as well, but his face was pretty much torn off. I'm guessing someone was particularly pissed at him."

Next to me Robbie gulped loudly. I asked, "What about out in the living room?"

"That was the daughter of the house, Silvia. She was the first victim. Seems to have been watching television at the time. No sign of forced entry, although the screens of the kitchen windows are busted out. The animals, whatever they were, got out that way. How they got in, though, is anyone's guess."

"You seem to vacillate between human and animal culprits."

Carson nodded unhappily. "Neighbor across the street saw two young men entering by the front entrance at eleven fifty precisely. One, according to her, was the son of the household, Matthew. She didn't know the other one, but she saw Matthew plainly. The porch light was on. The neighbor finished walking her dog and thought nothing more about it until she saw the squad cars arrive."

"She didn't hear anything?"

Shaking his head, Carson said, "No. Other than our anonymous informant, doesn't seem like anyone did. What happened here happened fast, probably too fast for the victims to scream. Now maybe you can shed some light on what *did* happen here."

"Before I do that—and let me just warn you, you're not going to like it—can I ask one question?"

Carson glowered, but he said, "Shoot."

"Do you happen to know where Matthew Elliot worked?"

Carson pulled out his notebook and consulted it. "We haven't got very far with this yet, naturally, but according to the lady walking the dog, he worked at a car repair shop. Smitty's Autobody."

Bingo. I was assuming our pack were all employees of Brandon Lewis. Now I was sure of it. I wanted to pat Carson reassuringly on the back, but I didn't think he'd appreciate the effort. "What you're dealing with here is a werewolf attack."

There was a time when Dave Carson would have blown up at hearing such a pronouncement and told me I was crazy. He knew better now, although he did look at me hopefully. "Please tell me you're kidding."

"Wish I were."

"You mean like Lon Chaney, late-night movie werewolves? Guys sprouting fur, that kind of thing?"

"Well, they don't really look much like old Lon, and it was Junior who played the wolf man, by the way."

Carson didn't seem impressed by my cinema knowledge. He was still obsessing over lycanthropy. "How the hell am I supposed to deal with werewolves?"

"You don't," I told him.

"That's where we come in," Robbie added.

CHAPTER 11

THERE WAS a moon out. Not a full one, thank you very much, but enough of one to provide some light.

Not that, as I told Carson, a full moon was needed. Hell, Brandon Lewis wolfed out and slashed my door while the sun was high in the sky. The bastard.

Robbie and I parked the car several blocks away and made our way through the back alley to the rear of Brandon's house. It was just about three in the morning. Somewhere nearby a dog was barking. No one seemed to pay it any attention.

As soon as we came through the fence gate and into the yard, Robbie had the gun I bought him out and ready, as instructed. I didn't think we'd find anyone at home, but there was no reason not to be prepared.

I'd have felt better if Elton could have joined us, but he didn't respond to my calls. Probably out doing demon things. Or maybe finding another rat to adopt.

There was no light on in the old house. The neighboring houses were similarly dark and quiet. Robbie and I walked through the overgrown lawn and up the stone steps leading to the back door. Just for shits and giggles, I tried the knob. It was locked.

Luckily I brought my handy-dandy housebreaking kit along with me. Robbie held a flashlight so I could get a better gander at what I was doing, so in under a minute, I had the door open. It creaked like a coffin in an old horror movie.

"It would," Robbie muttered.

We crept inside, both of us using flashlights now. We were in the kitchen, which was in need of a good cleaning, from what we could see. The kitchen table had several Domino's Pizza boxes stacked on it. Robbie opened one, and there was the remains of a cheese pizza that looked several days old.

"Let's not spend longer than we have to here," I whispered. "A desk or something is our best bet. Get any info we can and get out of here."

I figured Lewis and clan were holed up somewhere, maybe on the outskirts of the city. Hopefully he left a clue as to where they were. They certainly weren't spending any time at work, as the shop was still closed.

"Why are we whispering, if you're so sure no one is here?" Robbie asked in a barely audible tone.

"Because I'm not one hundred percent sure. Plus it adds to the drama."

Robbie agreed with that, and we made our way through the house until we found what seemed to be Brandon Lewis's bedroom. It wasn't exactly fit for a king. The mattress wasn't even on a frame, the bed just on the floor, shoved against the wall and covered with a few ratty blankets. A full plastic ashtray was on the floor next to the bed, as well as several beer cans.

"Lovely," Robbie said. "Frat-boy chic."

There was a desk against one wall, covered with papers, and yet another ashtray littered with butts. "I'll check here," I told Robbie, not bothering to whisper now that we knew Lewis wasn't at home. "You take a peek in his closet."

"What am I looking for?" Robbie asked.

"See if you can tell if he's taken a lot of his clothes. Although from the way he keeps house, that may be impossible to tell."

While Robbie rooted around, I sat down at the desk and sifted through the junk on top first. A lot of the pages seemed to have been torn from a notebook and were covered with a nearly illegible scrawl. From the looks of it, Brandon Lewis was a poet, and not a very good one. My flashlight beam came across one entitled *I Am the Moon*. I scanned down to the end, which was almost readable.

"Follow me, for I am strength
I am life and the bringer of destruction

You will bow down to me
And come to know my power.

"Those who cross me will shake with fear
Those who hate me will regret their ire
Those who battle me will scream as they die
For tonight death comes under a blood-red moon."

"Find anything?" Robbie asked as he rooted through Lewis's clothes.

"Nothing to worry Dylan Thomas." I grabbed another stack. More poems. An electric bill. A photograph showing Lewis and some scantily clad woman, both of them wearing cowboy hats. It seemed to have been taken at a park. There was a weatherworn picnic table in the background. Lewis had his arm around the woman, his attitude equal parts protection and ownership. I slipped the picture into my back pocket.

More poems. Something that could have been a grocery list. And a credit card statement.

"Got something," I announced.

Robbie turned from the closet. "Good, because all his clothes reek of cigarette smoke. What did you find?"

I held the bill aloft. "In the last month, Lewis has made a lot of charges at places in Clarks Hill, which tells me he's been spending a lot of time there. Maybe that's where we'll find him."

Clarks Hill was a small town up near Lafayette, about forty miles away. I'd never been there, but maybe it was time for a visit.

I stood up just as Robbie froze and signaled for me not to make any noise. I listened and heard what he must have: a car pulling into the driveway. We both immediately killed our flashlight beams, went to the window, and cautiously looked out. From our vantage point, we could only see a part of the drive, but the window was open, and we could hear the closing of car doors and muffled talking. Two shadowy figures came into view, moving to the front door. One was big, obviously my friend Brandon. The other was a very short guy, but I couldn't pick up any details of his face. As they came closer, I could hear their conversation.

"What are we going to do about him?" the short guy asked.

Brandon sighed heavily and paused to fish keys out of his pocket. "He's becoming unreliable. He'll have to be dealt with."

"I told you he'd never go along with it. He's a pussy."

They disappeared from sight as they climbed the porch steps, but I heard Brandon's reply. "Yeah, you were right. It's a shame, really. I can't believe anyone wouldn't want this gift."

Were they talking about Graig Betz? I thought it likely.

The front door squeaked as they opened it. I turned to Robbie, and in the light from the moon, I could see worry in his face. I wasn't exactly feeling calm myself.

Robbie already had his gun in his hand. I got mine out of the holster, and we both pointed them toward the doorway.

We could hear the two men moving about and chatting downstairs. Their voices weren't as clear now, but they didn't seem to be saying anything of importance. I picked up something about cigarettes and getting some booze. The short guy seemed to be doing all the talking. His voice was low and gruff.

The dilemma Robbie and I found ourselves in didn't leave us with many options. As we'd made our way through the house, I noticed that the floorboards creaked with nearly every step. I didn't fancy our chances getting out of the bedroom without making our presence known. Maybe Lewis and Short Guy wouldn't come upstairs. If they did, at least we were armed and had Gina's charms around our necks.

I took a few tentative steps. No creaks, but at that rate, I'd make it to a hiding place by Christmas. A quick glance at Robbie told me he was waiting to follow my lead, so I signaled for him to follow me, and together we moved—shuffled would be a more accurate term—over to the closet. In seconds we were inside, ducking behind the hanging clothes. Robbie was right. They reeked of cigarette smoke.

We left the closet door open just a smidgen. I hoped if they came upstairs they wouldn't need a change of clothes. It wasn't that I was worried Gina's charms wouldn't work, or that between Robbie and me, we couldn't wound them with some silver bullets, but I wanted to find Graig Betz, and I hoped they'd talk enough to lead me to him.

There was more muffled conversation, but it was getting closer and more audible and was now accompanied by the sound of creaking wood. Lewis and his buddy were coming up the stairs. I heard the short guy saying something about a pack of Winstons, and then the duo came into the bedroom. I was sure Robbie couldn't see any better than I could, what with hangers and shirts in our way, but at least we could hear them plainly now.

"Your laptop isn't here," said the short guy.

More creaking of floorboards and a shadow passed before the closet.

"I must have left it on the bed."

"I don't see it."

I heard the blankets being moved about, and then Lewis barked out a laugh. "It was buried. Here it is."

"I still don't see why we have to hide out at Ashley's or why we had to close up the shop."

"I told you, Myles, things are getting too hot." Lewis sounded like he was barely containing an explosion. "First that private detective shows up, and then that stupid stunt that Matt and Ray pulled last night—"

"Matt's always had a temper."

The short guy, Myles, seemed to be trying to assuage Lewis. Was there bad blood amongst the ranks?

There was a loud thump, and I assumed Lewis had smacked the wall. He seemed the wall-smacking type.

"We're not ready yet. We can't be calling attention to ourselves like that. The police are one thing. They're never going to believe that Matt's family were killed by a couple of werewolves. That detective guy, though, that Duncan Andrews, he's something different. He's dangerous."

"So you keep saying." Myles didn't sound worried about me. Little fucker.

"His place was protected. There was a spell of some kind, I tell you, that wouldn't let me in. It felt like there was an invisible electric fence around his apartment."

There was a pause, and then I heard Myles sniff. "Do you smell that?"

"What?"

Footsteps, presumably Myles's, came closer to the closet.

"Some kind of cologne. Someone's been in here."

Werewolves had an increased sense of smell, even when they weren't transformed. I looked over at the dark shape next to me, and sensed more than saw Robbie stiffen. I could barely smell it myself, but there was just a trace of the Polo I bought him for his birthday in the air.

I could almost hear the smile on Brandon Lewis's face as he said, "Oh my. Someone has come to call." He sniffed loudly. "You're right. And a soapy sort of smell as well. Shampoo, maybe? Someone's cleaned up nicely. And they're still here, if I'm not mistaken."

If our scent hadn't given us away, eventually they'd have heard one of us taking a breath. The thing about hiding and trying to keep from breathing loudly is eventually you exhale or something just a little too forcefully. I was tired of the closet in any case. Assuming Robbie still had his magnum in hand, I kicked the door open.

It shouldn't have taken them by surprise, and to be fair, Lewis was expecting something. Little Myles, though, seemed disoriented by two armed guys emerging from behind some hanging shirts. He froze in place. A wicked grin, however, crossed Lewis's face.

"Come to play, have we?" the big guy said. And then he transformed.

I'd seen guys turn into werewolves before, and it seemed there was no one set way. Some did it slowly, with the hair sprouting out on their arms and cheeks before the muscles and bones started to change. Some were quicker, and within seconds, they went from man to beast. I'd never seen anyone change as fast as Brandon Lewis, though. One moment he was standing by the bed, a muscular human wearing a tank top that revealed one sizable chest and tattoos almost covering his left arm. The next he was one big fucking werewolf. The clothing Lewis was wearing just shredded and ripped away as the transformation took place. And just to show he wasn't happy to see us, Lewis snarled and bared his fangs. He saw Robbie was taking a bead on him, and dodged to the left.

Robbie fired, but he hadn't braced himself, and the recoil sent him back a pace. He also hadn't aimed, at least not well. The bullet hit the wall close to Lewis's shoulder.

The sound of a gun going off in a small space didn't sit well with the human ear. Momentarily deafened, I aimed my .38 at Lewis, but he was fast. I expected him to charge at us, but instead he made for the window. I pulled the trigger, but I fared worse than Robbie did, hitting a mirror that was hanging on the wall near the window. Bad luck for me. Good luck for Lewis. The window was open, so all Lewis had to do was smash through the storm window. As it was he was so big he barely fit through the space.

Myles became a wolf as well, but his transformation took a little longer than Lewis's. When Lewis changed, his body grew rapidly as muscles and sinew enlarged. Myles stayed roughly the same size, so where there was once a guy wearing a basketball shirt with the number forty-two on it, there was now a werewolf wearing the jersey. It was a somewhat odd sight, seeing a werewolf wearing white socks and Nikes. No wonder they usually stripped naked before changing. It was hard to take a monster seriously when he reminded you of Michael J. Fox in *Teen Wolf.* Thank God it was dim in the room and I couldn't really get a good look at him. Otherwise I might have laughed.

I figured he'd head for the window as well, which would have been his downfall. He wasn't as close to it as Lewis had been, and I knew I'd have time to nail him. Instead, though, he made for the bedroom door.

He was out in the hall, ready to charge out of sight, when I shot him in the thigh.

The creature slammed against the wall, howling in pain. He slid to the floor, clutching at his leg. As he fell the transformation began. The fur covering his body receded and his facial features changed, animallike to human. I could hear the bones cracking and shifting as Myles went from werewolf to plain old Myles. By the time he was writhing on the floor, there wasn't any trace of the wolf left in him.

"You fucking bastard," he growled through gritted teeth, "you shot me." He was desperately holding his thigh, trying to staunch the flow of blood.

"Yeah," I said. "I guess I did."

Robbie and I moved out into the hall and stood over him. I reached over and flicked on the light switch so we could get a better look at the young man's damaged leg.

It wasn't too bad, although I don't think Myles would agree with that assessment. The bullet went through the back of his leg, the meaty part. There was a lot of blood, which was now covering Myles's upper leg, his hands, and a good section of the hall carpeting. Myles looked to be in his early twenties, with pale skin, long dirty-blond hair, and a scraggly beard. His arms were covered with tats, and the parts of his chest that showed indicated there were more there. He sort of reminded me of a hobbit, if a hobbit decided to dress for a game of hoops.

"I can't... I can't change back," Myles whimpered.

I shook my head. "Nope."

There were tears in his eyes as he looked up at us. "Help me. I'm dying."

"You're really not," I told him.

Robbie put his gun in its holster, which he wore on his hip, and got down next to Myles to examine the wound closer. He gently moved Myles's hands so he could see. "Looks like the bullet went straight through. Didn't even hit the bone. Good shooting, Dunc."

"Thanks."

Myles let out a whimper. "I'm fucking bleeding to death."

Robbie gave him a stern look. "Suck it up, Wolf Boy. You'll live. Try dying in a car crash some time. Now *that* was a bitch!"

CHAPTER 12

"I CAN'T believe I missed," Robbie groused. "He was, what, maybe eight feet away from me? I mean, yeah, he moved like Speedy Gonzales, but still…."

We were back at our apartment, sitting on the couch, cuddled up and thinking about our warm, soft bed just down the hall. I think we were both too tired to make the trip, though. Daisy was curled up next to Robbie, sighing contentedly. Robbie was plastered against me, nearly dead weight, talking into my chest with his arm around my neck. It would have been okay with me if we never moved again.

"Have I ever told you about the O.K. Corral?" I said, Robbie's thick black hair almost getting in my mouth as I spoke. I puffed to blow a tuft away from my lips.

"You're not that old," Robbie said.

I ignored the feeble joke. "Despite being known as the gunfight at the O.K. Corral, the event actually took place in a small patch of land outside a photographic studio. When it started, the two parties were only about six feet apart from each other. In thirty seconds, over thirty shots were fired. Of the seven guys involved in the shootout, three were killed, two were wounded, Doc Holliday was grazed, and Wyatt Earp walked away without a scratch on him."

"And this is supposed to make me feel better how?"

I smiled gently, even though from his vantage point, Robbie couldn't see it. "Just that it's not easy to shoot another human being, especially if he's up close. Something in your brain tries to stop you.

After a while you can teach yourself to override this, but the first few times.... I'm just saying you did good. Hell, my first shootout, the guy was closer than Lewis was to you, and he might as well have been in Poughkeepsie for all the good my aim was."

I was holding Robbie close, and I could feel the muscles in his shoulders relax a little.

"I suppose," he muttered.

"Plus that was one fast fucking werewolf." There were several things about Brandon Lewis that bothered me. One was the transformation itself. Too quick. I'd never seen someone who could wolf out in two seconds flat. And then there was his size. I mean, Lewis was hardly a stick figure, but in wolf form, he was enormous. The speed he possessed bothered me as well. I couldn't blame Robbie for missing what was essentially a blur.

"My ears still hurt," Robbie said, snuggling even tighter against me.

"That's something they never tell you on television cop shows. Firing a gun inside, especially in a small room, doesn't do wonders for your hearing. It'll pass."

"What do you think will happen to our buddy Myles?"

I thought back to the scene in the upstairs hall of Brandon Lewis's house. Myles Sprouse, according to his driver's license, wasn't helpful when we tried to get information out of him. For some reason he seemed more anxious to get his wound attended to. Some people! Robbie and I discussed bringing him to Gina, who could have eased his pain and mixed a brew that would increase his healing time to a mere few days, but after a few minutes of chatting with him, we decided against it. He wasn't a pleasant young man.

"Fuck you," he'd said more than once. "When Brandon gets hold of you, there won't be enough pieces left for the police to put together."

This put an image of Lieutenant Carson trying to piece me together like a jigsaw puzzle in my head, which amused me in an odd way.

I did show Myles the pic of Lewis and the woman. "Who's the gal?" I asked.

"Never seen her before," Myles growled. He winced right after that. "Why can't I change?"

"You're cured, buddy boy. No more wolf for you."

He sneered at this news. "I'll just have Brandon bite me again."

"I wouldn't do that. With the cure coursing through your veins, it might do nasty things to you. Like kill you." Although I wasn't sure if that would be horribly bad. I tried another tactic. "So tell me about Brandon. How is it that he's like some sort of super wolf? What's his secret?"

For an answer Myles called me several names I hadn't heard since middle school, and even brought my mother into it. So I patted him on the leg, right near his wound. This made him howl with pain.

"We're going to go now," I told him. "We'll call an ambulance for you. Tell them you shot yourself because you realized you're an ass."

And we left him there in the hallway, bleeding and cursing our parentage.

Robbie raised his head off my chest, snapping me out of my reverie. Suddenly he seemed more awake and even a little frisky. He favored me with a sly smile.

"Feel like doing nasty things with each other's genitalia?"

My eyelids were heavy, and the thought of moving even an inch away from where we were filled me with dread. But it was Robbie.

"You bet," I replied.

I WENT out to lunch with Nick. Robbie stayed home to do research, such as checking out Brandon Lewis's Facebook page (if he had one) and stuff like that. Plus, since he stopped being a ghost and became one of us boring living people, Robbie didn't seem to like being around Nick much. It wasn't that they didn't like each other, but their history was... weird. I think both of them were slightly uncomfortable in the other's company. Also I still didn't like Robbie going out too much during the day, as it was always possible someone who knew him back before he died might spot him, and we also had a litter of werewolves wanting to tear us limb from limb. Inside was a good place for Robbie, where Gina's hexes would protect him. I didn't tell him this, of course.

After lunch Nick and I ended up strolling around downtown, just shooting the shit as we walked. We ended up at the Soldiers and Sailors

Monument, where we sat on the steps and watched people and the traffic going around the Circle.

"This is nice," Nick said. "Seems like ages since we've spent any time together, just you and me."

"I hadn't noticed," I said.

He knew I was lying through my teeth and chuckled.

"Well, you've been with Casey a lot lately. How's that going?"

Nick thought about his answer a moment. "Pretty well. We really just enjoy each other's company. Don't really talk about our special abilities much. Hell, I'm not sure I even really understand his."

"Your gifts shouldn't really enter into it. You either like each other or you don't. If he can chat with certain people without opening his mouth, who cares? If you can see spirits, what does it matter? Hell, I'd think it would bond the two of you, if anything. Someone who understands the difficulties that come with paranormal skills."

Nick rested his elbows on his knees and held his chin in his hands as he watched the cars go by. "I can turn it on and off now, you know."

I didn't. "That's good," I said.

"It got too… difficult. It was so hard, seeing ghosts everywhere I went. There were too many, and it was painful knowing I couldn't help all of them. I can't believe how many people die and can't seem to move on." He turned his head, watching the people walking around us, taking pictures of the monument or the statues around it. "Like right now. I'm sure there are ghosts close by, but I can't see them."

I didn't see any, but I didn't want to spoil the moment by pointing it out. So I shifted the conversation back to Nick's budding relationship. "I like Casey," I said. "He's nice. And hot. Really, really hot. I like that whole skin-like-milk-chocolate thing he's got going."

Nick chuckled, slightly embarrassed by my description. "I'm not sure, but that could be taken as racist. Isn't comparing people of color to candy bars not considered PC?"

Damn it, he was right. And here I'd always considered myself an enlightened guy, one who didn't give a crap about the color of a person's skin. I mentally berated myself and awkwardly tried to rescue the conversation. "Well," I said, flushing, "that's true. Very true. Spot on. You're right. Sorry. But the rest stands. I like him. He's likable. Very likable. And hot. Lickable. Very likable." Okay, going too far now. Don't sound like you're making a play for Nick's new guy. Jesus, why was talking about your friend's new beau so difficult?

"He is at that." Nick nodded and looked over at a woman taking a selfie with the statue of William Henry Harrison behind her. Luckily he didn't seem to think I was being an ass. Well, no more than usual. "He's very likeable. And lickable. In fact, I have. Several times now, in fact." He paused. "I think I'm falling in love with him."

I patted Nick's knee. "That's fantastic! I'm really pleased. He seems like a great guy."

Nick flushed with embarrassment. "Yeah. Well, enough about me. What have you been up to lately?"

"Well, let's see. I killed a Gorgon. That's pretty big. Oh, and I'm hunting down a pack of werewolves, one of whom is one big badass motherfu—"

"Wait. You killed a Gorgon? One of those ladies with snakes coming out of their heads?"

"Just like on the brochures. Luckily for me she was wearing a hood at the time. Otherwise I could be out there with William Henry Harrison, doing the statue thing. But I—"

My cell phone rang. I got it out of my pocket and answered without checking the incoming phone number. "Yep. What you need?"

I assumed it would be Robbie, but the voice was definitely not his. Instead I heard Brandon Lewis's dark, gruff tones.

"I'm going to give you one warning, man. Stay away from me and my clan."

Nick was still sitting on the steps right next to me, and people were walking around the monument, chatting and laughing. My entire world, however, was just a voice on the telephone. No one else existed at the moment. "'Clan' isn't really the word, is it?" I tried to sound casual, like the sound of his voice didn't chill me to the bone. "'Pack' is more apt, wouldn't you say?"

"We're not to be messed with. Just ask the Elliot family."

"Yeah, but that wasn't your idea, was it? You forget I overheard you and Myles. Matthew Elliot and another of your boys went rogue, didn't they? The slaughter of that family wasn't part of your plan. How is Myles, by the way? Have you heard from him?"

"He's with us." The anger in Lewis's voice was palpable. "I think he's dying. And you'll pay for that."

I frowned, wondering if Myles was even picked up by the ambulance Robbie and I summoned.

Lewis went on, answering my unasked question. "I went back for him. Got there just before the EMTs arrived. He couldn't change, but I got him out without being seen."

"And you've bitten him again." My God. What was happening in that young man's body now? Gina's cure mixing with a fresh werewolf bite would be waging a war on a cellular level. And Myles Sprouse was losing.

"You're going to suffer for what you did to him."

I decided to be flip. Make your opponent angry enough to start making mistakes. It'd worked for me in the past. "First you tell me to leave you and your doggies alone. Then you start making threats. Which is it going to be? If you're gunning for me, believe me, I'm prepared—"

"Your partner," Lewis said. "The one you were with last night. I'm going to flay him alive. Tie him up and just slice him slowly. His death will be agonizing. And I'm going to make you watch."

I stood up, only vaguely aware Nick was looking at me anxiously. He could tell the phone call wasn't pleasant. "Listen to me, you son of a bitch—"

"No," Lewis said, "you listen to me. You don't know what you're dealing with. I know you've got some magic working for you. The protective spells at your apartment. Silver bullets that keep my kind from transforming. And I felt something last night as well, that you were safeguarded in some way. Well, you can only hide behind your magic spells for so long, Andrews. I'll break through them, and then everyone you love will die. I guarantee that."

"You—" I stopped when I realized he'd hung up. Immediately I tried Robbie's number. No answer.

Nick got to his feet. "What's up?"

I was already moving, walking down the steps. Well, running, really. "Got to get home," I said, "and check on Robbie."

I BURST into the apartment so fast Daisy didn't even have time to jump off the couch to run and greet me. Robbie was sitting at his desk, typing away on his laptop. He turned with a smile, which quickly faded as he saw my worried state. He stood and frowned just as I got to him and wrapped him in my arms.

"I'm glad to see you too, Dunc," he said, obviously uncertain as to what was going on.

I squeezed him tight, and we swayed a little as we stood there. "I just had to know you were safe."

"An army of werewolves couldn't get through that door," he said. "About the only thing that could is a ghost, since Gina's spells don't work well on—"

"Humans. Humans can get through," I said. "And most of the time, Brandon Lewis and his gang are human. Luckily for me he hasn't thought of that. The only time he tried to get in, he'd changed to wolf form before attempting entry."

Robbie moved back, holding me at arm's length. "Yeah, but it's not exactly like I'm going to let him in, is it? And I've had the door locked the whole time you've been gone."

"From now on," I said seriously, "keep it bolted as well. Just to be sure." Briefly I filled him in on Lewis's phone call.

"Sounds like you've got him rattled," he said.

"Maybe too much. I don't want people hurt before I have a chance to deal with him."

Robbie snapped his fingers. "Speaking of which, I've found a lot of info about the leader of our werewolf pack." He turned to his laptop, bending over to hit a few keys. "If you're going to be a supernatural baddie with intentions of ripping people to shreds, it might be a good idea *not* to have a Facebook page."

The screen Robbie brought up was indeed Brandon Lewis's Facebook profile. "I can't believe he still has one," I said.

"And I checked his friends list. Sure enough we have Myles Sprouse, Matthew Elliot, and Kelvin Hicks, all of whom are employees of Smitty's Autobody. Lewis said last night that Matt and a guy named Kel had attacked the Elliot family. I'm guessing Kel is Kelvin."

"Makes sense."

"And our friend Myles said something about hiding out at Ashley's. Well, look here." Robbie moved the cursor over to where it listed Brandon Lewis's relationship status. "Seems Lewis and one Ashley Campbell are a couple. And we click on Ashley's name…."

Another page came up, belonging to the woman in question. Robbie, hunched over the desk, tapped a few more keys until he found a good picture of Ashley Campbell. She was definitely the woman in the cowboy hat in the picture I found on Lewis's desk.

"I don't suppose you also conveniently found her address and that she lives in or near Clarks Hill, did you?"

Robbie made a sour face. "Actually her town here is listed as Mishawaka, but she might have moved and just never updated. I wonder if—"

He was interrupted by a knock at our door. The rhythm was a special one Gina used, but I looked out the peephole before opening, just to be safe. She breezed in, talking as soon as she crossed the threshold.

"Tell me again why I wanted to be a teacher." Gina had one of those pop-open umbrellas dangling from her wrist, and the string had tangled with one of her bracelets. The forecast threatened rain, but so far the promise was unfulfilled. She struggled to get the cord free, but the tangled umbrella didn't impede the flow of words. "Little monsters are what they are, and some of them aren't so little. You wouldn't believe how many papers I'll have to grade over the weekend, and—"

She stopped as she saw the screen on Robbie's laptop. "Oh my God," she said.

"Yeah," Robbie said, a little proud of his findings. "We've located our werewolf's girlfriend. One Ashley Campbell."

Gina arched an eyebrow and moved closer to the desk. "Is that what she's calling herself these days? The last time I saw her she was still going by Sondra Benoit."

"You know her?" I asked.

"Oh yes." Gina sat down on Robbie's chair and stared at the Facebook page. "At one time, quite well. If she's mixed up with Brandon Lewis, then we're in big trouble. Really big trouble."

I knew what the answer would be, but I had to ask anyway. "Why is that?"

Gina turned to me, her face stony. "Because she's a witch."

CHAPTER 13

"LAST I knew she lived in Mishawaka," Gina said. "Same face. She's had that one for at least fifty years, although she's made it a little younger now."

We were in the park, and it was dusk. Robbie was off with Daisy, making sure she didn't get too close to anyone getting ready to leave the park. The squirrel blood and gray matter around her jowls might upset them. Gina and I ambled around, finally ending up on a small wooden bridge over a creek. She leaned against the railing and gazed at the sky.

"She's a little older than me. And not, if I may say so, a very nice person."

I nodded. "She doesn't seem to have picked nice friends."

"Sondra, or Ashley as she goes by now, is a totem witch. The closest thing I can compare her to in your culture would be a voodoo priestess, or at least Hollywood's depiction of a voodoo priestess. It wouldn't surprise me to find that she is behind Brandon Lewis being a werewolf. It also explains why he's not your typical werewolf."

"She's upped his wolfie-ness."

Gina folded her arms and shivered. It wasn't a cold night, so it wasn't the weather that made her quiver. "She'll be working on ways to get past our defenses. I don't think we can count on the charms working for much longer."

"How about the bullets?"

"That will take her longer to figure out, I think."

"Still, we're going to have to move fast."

"Oh yes."

I looked to see if I could spot Daisy and Robbie. They weren't in sight, but there was a soccer game breaking up, so I ogled some guys in shorts instead. None of them had anything on Robbie, but I gave one guy a mental consolation prize. When he vanished from view, I returned to the conversation. "Are we ready for this?"

Gina curled her lip. "Probably not. But it's never stopped us before."

We both grinned at that, mainly because it was true, but before I could come up with something witty in reply, my cell phone rang.

It was a number I didn't recognize, so I answered with just my name. "Mr. Andrews, this is Laura. Laura Johnson."

Despite having chatted with the stripper only a few days previously, it took me a second to realize I was talking to Graig Betz's old girlfriend. I didn't expect to hear back from her, so I guess I shoved her right out of my mind. "How can I help you, Laura?"

There was a short silence, and I wondered for a moment if I'd lost the connection. Finally, though, she said in a small voice, "Graig is here, Mr. Andrews. He's here with me. And... I'm scared."

"Are you okay? Is he threatening you?"

She was flustered, but she got it out. "No, he's with me. We're.... They're after us, Mr. Andrews. His friends. I think they want to kill us."

My mind raced, and I could picture another scene like I witnessed at the Elliot household. I didn't know where "here" was, but wherever Laura and Graig were, it wouldn't be safe enough. I asked Laura for her address, and she gave it. It was on the near east side, she told me. About ten minutes away from us, fifteen if traffic was bad.

"Okay, here's what I want you to do," I said. "Get out of your apartment immediately. Is there a place nearby with a lot of people?"

"There's a bar just down the block. Western Annie's."

"Go there. We'll meet you there as soon as possible."

It was a good thing I didn't promise to arrive at a certain time because it actually took us nearly half an hour before we parked in the lot across the street from Western Annie's. Friday night traffic in Indianapolis was never a walk in the park, but when you added in some event downtown—a basketball game, football game, whatever—it was much, much worse. Still, there were no screams of panic coming from inside the tavern and no hordes of people exiting with blood all over them, so I assumed we'd arrived in time.

Robbie stayed in the car with Daisy while Gina and I went in.

Annie's was crowded and dark, and until my eyes adjusted, all I could make out was a long bar with people all around it, several TVs showing a boxing match, and loads of very drunk people, mostly men. When I got accustomed to the lighting, things didn't change all that much, although now I could see a lot of the very drunk men were wearing western shirts and cowboy hats. Merle Haggard was playing on the jukebox, and a few guys were huddled around the Wurlitzer, singing along. The place was noisy and smelled of beer and sweat. We showed our IDs to a guy at the door, who let us in and told us to have a good time. He didn't sound sincere.

A couple of young bucks wearing ball caps wolf whistled at Gina as she walked by them. She gave them a sweet smile, and one yelled, "Hey, honey, can I buy you a beer?"

She stopped long enough to tap him on the lips with her forefinger. "Maybe another time, sweetie."

Ball Cap and his buddies were sitting on bar stools that were against the wall, and I guessed it was prime real estate at Annie's to sit there, as one could check out everyone coming in. One of the guys tried to put his arm around Gina's waist and pull her close, but she muttered a few words and twirled her finger in the air. The stool the guy was sitting on suddenly moved, mimicking her motion exactly. Seconds later the guy was trying to figure out how he'd slipped off his bar stool and spilled beer all over himself.

Gina just smiled to herself. "Drunks," she said so only I could hear, "they're so easy."

I spotted Laura at the corner of the bar, and she had her arms protectively around a young black man I recognized from his photo as Graig Betz.

He wasn't exactly what I was expecting, but it was hard to go by one photograph sometimes. He was only average height, and I'd pictured tall. From the picture I got a badass vibe, someone you wouldn't want to mess with, and while I was sure that was somewhere within Graig, it wasn't showing now. Now he looked frightened and soft, someone you wanted to step in front of and say "Move aside, sir. I'll take care of this now" before you blew Godzilla away with your bazooka.

Graig had a pencil-thin mustache, the kind Vincent Price used to wear, and a very trimmed, barely there beard that followed the line of his jaw perfectly. His skin was a few shades lighter than his grandmother's, and he had a tattoo of a snake on his left bicep. He was wearing a white tank top so the tat was plainly visible. It must have been a rule at Smitty's Autobody. Only wear tank tops or basketball jerseys. We must show off our biceps and impress the ladies.

Laura sighed with relief when I approached. "Thank God you're here," she said, barely audible with Merle blasting in my ears. "I was afraid…."

While she thought about what she was afraid of, Graig extricated himself from her embrace and stood to offer me his hand. "Mr. Andrews," he said, "it's a pleasure to meet you."

His voice had a soft quality to it as well, and I would bet the farm (if I had one) he butched it up for his buddies at work. That, or his nickname around the garage was Squeaky. Good handshake, though. It's always nice to get a firm grasp that didn't become a macho battlefield.

"Likewise," I told him. "But first things first. Do you know where Lewis and his buddies are right now?"

Graig shook his head. "Looking for me, I expect."

Laura put her arm back around Graig and held him close. "They know he don't want no part of this."

The story would have to wait. For one, it was much too crowded in Annie's to converse, and shouting about werewolves and blood and killing in a bar was frowned upon in most etiquette books. Lewis and other members of the pack might be close by, which was another reason to skedaddle.

Gina had hung back, letting me make contact with the couple on my own, but now she stepped up next to me. I introduced her, saying only she was a friend and she was there to help. Laura ran her eye up and down Gina, and I knew she was wondering how a tiny slip of woman would be any use, but before she could say anything, Graig opened his eyes wide as he spotted someone behind us.

"Shit," he said. "It's Ray."

I turned to see a guy at the entrance who seemed to be scanning the crowd. A young guy, he was wearing the obligatory tank top, this one black, and had black hair cut very short on the side, longer on top. While he wasn't anywhere near Brandon Lewis in size, he still looked like he could handle himself in a scrap. Ray was ignoring the guy at the door who was checking IDs and just craning his neck to get a gander at the crowd.

"Ray?" I asked Graig.

He nodded. "Ray Smith. He's one of them."

Ray probably wasn't old enough to be in Western Annie's, which was why he and the ID guy weren't getting along so well. I couldn't hear what Ray was saying, but lip reading it seemed he was telling ID guy to chill out, that he was just looking for someone. ID guy wasn't buying it and was telling Ray to leave. He even opened the door to usher Ray out.

Ray took one last look and spotted us. A smile spread across his face. The smile said it all. Gotcha.

"Come on," I told Laura and Graig. "Let's get out of here."

"But he's seen us!" Laura protested.

"He won't do anything here," I said. "Too many people around."

I sincerely hoped that was true.

We pushed our way back through the crowd and got to the exit. We filed out, first me and Gina, followed by Laura and Graig. Ray was waiting for us outside, a few paces away, looking calm and cool. He ignored me and nodded at Graig.

"We been looking for you, man," he said.

"I don't got nothing to say to you, Ray," Graig replied.

When we tried to walk on, Ray moved into our path. He moved with the easy grace of a natural fighter and stood inches away from my face. We were roughly the same height. I stared right into his dark eyes. They always said not to let them smell fear on you. I wondered how good they were with sniffing apprehension.

"I know you," Ray said with a sneer. "You're the private dick." He overpronounced the last word to give it added meaning.

I smiled. "That's me."

"Fucking faggot from what I hear." He oscillated his head slightly, like a cobra about to strike.

I patted him on the shoulder. He immediately shrugged it off, but I kept the grin on my face. "Sorry, but I'm already taken."

Ray was so angry I could see the veins sticking out on his neck. "I ought to fucking slice you right now, you pervert."

"I don't think that would be a good idea," I told him.

There were a few people out on the sidewalk, walking either to Annie's or to other joints nearby. A few people glanced uneasily our way, wondering if a fight was going to break out. Two guys in cowboy hats hurried past us into the relatively safe confines of Western Annie's.

I didn't take my eyes off Ray, but I sensed Gina at my side and knew Laura and Graig were right behind me. Hell, I could almost feel the worry wafting off Laura. The atmosphere was tense, and I was afraid Ray might do something stupid like throw caution to the wind and change into a werewolf right then and there, pedestrians be damned.

He seemed to think it a good possibility too. "Why the fuck not?" he asked.

"Because," I said, nodding over to the parking lot across the street, "there's a guy in a car over there covering you with a .357 Magnum."

The fight in Ray's eyes wavered, and he shifted his gaze long enough to see Robbie hanging out of the passenger side window, gun in hand. Robbie waved at him. Ray didn't wave back. When he turned back to me, there was uncertainty in his manner. The anger and the fight were still there. He just didn't know where to direct them.

"We're going now," I told him. "I don't suggest following us. Go tell Brandon that we'll be coming for him."

Ray's lip quivered from having to contain his fury. "You're going to get yours, faggot," he snarled. "I'm going to gut you myself. Just wait."

"You've got the wrong haircut," I said.

That obviously confused him. "What?"

"Your ears stick out too much. When you keep your hair short on the sides like that, longer on top, it makes your ears stand out. You look a bit like Mickey Mouse. It's hard to feel threatened by a guy when all you can think is 'Jesus, look at those ears.'"

I stepped around him and walked on without glancing back, as if he wasn't worth a second glance. I heard Gina and the others following me. Ray grunted something at Graig I didn't catch in its entirety, but

Graig's reply suggesting Ray go fuck himself was fairly clear. I had to force myself to keep a slow pace as we crossed the street to the parking lot, and I admit I breathed a sigh of relief when we actually got to the car.

Robbie slid over to the driver's seat and gunned the engine as we climbed in, me in front and Gina in the back with Graig and Laura. Once the doors were shut, he pulled out of the lot with tires screaming.

Laura was behind Robbie, and I could see her put a hand to her heart as she panted. "Oh my God," she said breathlessly, "I can't believe…."

Apparently she had a habit of not finishing sentences. Now I'd never know what she didn't believe.

"I thought Ray was going to change for sure," Graig said.

I glanced up in the rear mirror to see him twisted around, checking out Ray's dwindling figure as we raced down the street.

"I thought so too. That's why I kept him discombobulated."

"Discombobulated?" Robbie asked, slowing down to take a turn. Even so we got a bit jostled, and the tires made more protesting sounds.

"It's a technical term," I said. "Keep your enemy off his toes so he doesn't change into a werewolf, causing a big old fight right outside a seedy bar."

"That the dictionary definition?"

Another turn. This time Robbie had reduced the speed enough that we made it without being tossed around. We almost clipped a Volkswagen, though, and the driver sounded his horn.

"Should be." I turned to look back at Graig and Laura to see if they were okay. They weren't. Both of them were shaking like rabbits that have realized they just walked into a coyote den.

"Where are we going?" Laura asked.

"The safest place in the world," I said.

Graig wasn't convinced by my words. "And where's that?" he demanded.

I couldn't see Gina, as she was seated behind me, but her voice was soft and had a calming effect.

"That would be my apartment," she said simply.

CHAPTER 14

GINA'S NEW place was on Massachusetts Avenue, which was known as the arts district of town. There was Theatre on the Square, a comedy club, and enough little artsy-fartsy shops to satisfy the Bohemian in anyone. There was also one of the larger gay nightclubs on Mass, a place called the Metro. Gina's apartment was above a little flower shop, and she had a good view of the entrance of the Metro from her living room window. She said she didn't pick the place for the sole reason of watching the young gaylings coming and going, but I didn't believe her.

I missed her old house, but the new digs had class and some extra added features. I wasn't kidding when I said it was the safest place on Earth. Not only was it charmed up to the hilt, but it was inhabited by a Netherbeing that was completely besotted with Gina. This creature—not really a ghost because it had never lived—had no form I could make out, but made its presence known by controlling the lights and speaking in a gruff voice.

Netherbeings were Earth spirits, if that made any sense, and had no actual gender, but as this one sounded astoundingly like Emma Stone being cross with someone, we referred to it as Emma.

I was right behind Gina as she entered the apartment, so I heard Emma's sigh of contentment as her favorite being returned home. For me and Robbie, Emma grunted, which was her way of saying we were acceptable, and she giggled for Daisy, but when Graig and Laura came in, the lighting dimmed immediately and there was thunder in her voice.

"Who dares to infiltrate my dwelling?"

The young couple froze in place, and Gina had to physically move them aside so she could close the door. "It's okay, Emma," she said breezily. "They're friends."

Emma wasn't convinced. "One of them is tainted."

"Yeah, well, I can take care of that," Gina replied.

The room felt hot and airless, and for a second, I thought Emma was going to stand firm, but then the lights came up a little and the mood abated.

"If you say so," Emma said.

There was a rustling in the walls, and I think Emma went away to sulk.

Laura looked like she might faint. "Your apartment *talks* to you?"

Gina smiled sweetly. "She does more than talk. If I hadn't convinced her that you were friends, she'd have crushed you to a pulp. Pretty protective, our Emma."

Graig and Laura were clutching each other tightly, and I could tell they were thinking they might have made a mistake, aligning themselves with us. I thought they needed reassurance, so I explained who Emma was, adding, "The great thing about having a Netherbeing here is that no one, and I mean no one, can enter without Emma's permission. She can keep out humans, ghosts, witches, werewolves, demons, and even zombie dogs if she chooses. They can't even sense that this place exists. So you're safe as long as you're within these walls."

By the worry in Graig's eyes, I wasn't sure I succeeded. "Ghosts? Witches?" he said.

"What, you're a werewolf. You can buy that, but ghosts and witches are too much for you?"

He took a deep breath and let it out. "I guess I just never really thought about it."

There hadn't been much talk on the ride to Gina's. For one thing Robbie kept his foot on the pedal, watching out for cops and pedestrians and other cars as much as possible, and it was hard to talk much when you were holding on for dear life. Daisy had taken a liking to Laura and climbed into her lap to comfort her. Laura commented on Daisy looking sickly, but that was about as paranormal as the conversation got. Mostly we said things like "slow down!" and "look out!" and "I think I'm going to be sick!" That last was Graig's contribution. Apparently transforming from man to wolf was not a problem, but car sickness was. Or maybe he was just casting aspersions about Robbie's driving skills, which, considering how out of practice he was, really weren't that bad.

We got Graig and Laura settled on the couch, and Gina disappeared into the kitchen to make some tea. Daisy remained close to Laura, who petted her nonstop while we waited. No one said anything. Gina came back bearing two mugs, which she handed to the young couple. To get hers, Laura had to release Graig's hand she'd been holding. There was no way the other hand was going to stop scratching Daisy behind the ears.

"This will calm you down," Gina promised.

I had no doubt it would, and in fact, after they took just a sip you could see a difference in the two. They no longer resembled scared rabbits. Laura drank some more and sighed heavily, like the weight of the world was coming off her shoulders.

Robbie and Gina picked seats away from the couple so they wouldn't feel crowded, but I moved a chair right up near them and sat down. "So," I said, "tell me what's going on."

"Brandon wants to kill me," Graig said.

"I gathered that. Why?"

The question seemed to confuse Graig. "Because... well, I...."

"Drink some more tea," I told him.

He did. "Sorry," he said, his voice steadier. "I guess I'm just a bit rattled, what with that guy's driving and then a talking room."

The lighting in the room brightened just a tad, and the Netherbeing said, "Call me Emma, if it helps. I've grown accustomed to the name."

Graig weakly wagged his fingers. "Hi, Emma."

"Hello, and welcome to this abode."

I was sure that, as a dancer at Pickin's, Laura had seen quite a lot in her time, but she was really having a hard time coping with the events of the evening. Luckily the tea was helping. I wondered what Gina put in it.

"I'm so confused," she muttered. It almost seemed like she was saying it to Daisy. Daisy looked up at her with her bloodshot eyes and let out a little huff, as if in agreement.

"Gina's marvelous," Emma gushed. "And you should feel honored to be here. Just to be in her presence...."

"Thanks, Emma," Gina said, not unkindly, "we can take it from here."
The lighting dimmed again.

I looked Graig in the eyes. I needed him to concentrate. "Tell me about Brandon."

He nodded slightly. "What do you want to know?"

"Everything."

Graig sat back on the couch, now looking thoroughly relaxed. "It's a long story."

I smiled. "We're not going anywhere."

"I don't even know where to start."

"The beginning is usually the best place. How did you meet Brandon Lewis?"

Graig almost laughed. The sound stuck in his throat, though, so he abandoned it. "A job interview. They had a help wanted sign out, so I went in. I know a bit about cars, so I thought I had a chance."

And slowly Graig told his tale. He began working at Smitty's along with Ray and Kel and the other guys. At first he felt like an outsider, being both the new guy and the only one who wasn't white, but he soon formed a friendship with Kelvin Hicks, who liked to work out and boxed a little bit. When Graig showed an interest, Kel took him to a gym, and they worked out a few times. Of all the guys at work, Matthew Elliot was the only one who worried Graig. Matt seemed too angry and sometimes came to work still drunk from the night before.

"And one day he let something slip," Graig said. "He was hungover and working on a simple oil change when he said it was stupid to be doing such mundane shit when they had such power. One of the other guys, I think it was Myles, tried to get him to shut his trap, but he kept on and said, 'I only feel truly alive now during the night. Hunting a fox or a deer. This shit's for the birds.' I thought it was weird. Hunting at night? Myles even said not to talk in front of me, which also made me curious. And then Kel said, 'It's time we made Graig one of us anyhow.'"

"And then they told you about the pack," I prompted.

"I thought they were crazy at first. But then Brandon took me aside and said he'd show me that night. Once we were done for the day, we went out to eat. I still thought they were pulling some big joke on me. But then we all piled into Ray's van and drove out to the country. Ended up in some big field, out in the middle of nowhere. I thought we were just going to get stoned and drink some beer or something."

Graig was a good storyteller. I'd give him that. I could picture the scene in my head.

GRAIG WAS slightly drunk and didn't really need another beer, but Kel pressed another bottle into his hands, and he didn't want to look like a pussy and refuse. Ray had stopped the van, pulled just barely off the road. Brandon was up front with Ray while the others were piled in the back along with a cooler full of brews. Brandon was laughing at something Ray said as he got out of the van. Matt Elliot opened the back door and jumped out, letting out a loud howl as his feet hit the dirt. Kel followed, taking off his shirt and tossing it back into the van.

Myles, seeing Graig was a little nervous, slapped his coworker on the back. "It'll be fine. Trust me."

Graig looked out the back of the van and wondered. Where the hell were they? There was a cornfield across the road, and Graig thought he could make out a farmhouse in the distance. Other than that there was no sign of civilization.

He set the beer down on the floor of the van, feeling suddenly sober. After all, he didn't know these guys all that well. Sure, Kel was all right, and Myles seemed okay, but Matt and Brandon seemed a little racist, as far as Graig was concerned. They joked about Graig being their token black, and while the comments were made in jest, Graig thought there was some animosity behind them. They didn't really trust him or even like him. He was the new guy and a darkie (a phrase Brandon used on more than one occasion). In his short life, Graig had worked many places. A fast food joint. A shoe store. A pizza restaurant. He'd never been the only black guy before, and he wasn't sure he liked it. It set him apart from the other guys.

And to be truthful, Matt Elliot worried Graig. There was something in Matt's eyes that just wasn't right. You could see the rage in the guy. He often complained about how much he hated his family and sometimes even talked about smacking his girlfriend around.

Matt just wasn't all there, in Graig's opinion.

And now Matt and Kel were standing out in the dirt behind the van, shirtless and pulling off their shoes and socks. What the hell was going on?

Now Brandon and Ray joined them. Ray had stripped down to his skivvies, having left the rest of his clothes on the front seat of the van. Brandon, still fully clothed, lit a cigarette and watched the others with a slight smile on his face. As Matt and Kel quickly undid their belts and began to pull off their jeans, Brandon peered into the back of the van. "You guys coming out, or what?"

"We're coming," Myles assured him, taking off his basketball jersey.

Graig chuckled uneasily. "I'm not sure I even know what's going on."

"Well, we're about to show you, aren't we?"

Brandon seemed to be mocking Graig, but in what way, Graig wasn't sure.

To ease the tension he felt, Graig made a feeble joke. "Is this some kind of back-to-nature thing?" He forced a chuckle.

"More than you can imagine," Brandon said.

Myles removed his shoes and socks, grinning at Graig mischievously. "It's freedom, man," he said. "Like you've never known before."

"I got to admit, you guys are confusing the hell out of me." Seeing Ray, Matt, and Kel tossing their underwear into the back of the van, Graig suppressed the urge to emit a nervous laugh. This wasn't some gay thing, was it? Not that Graig was homophobic. Hell, he'd been hit on by guys lots of times, and Graig usually took it as a compliment (except for that old guy, and he was just creepy). Doing it with guys just wasn't Graig's thing, and from the jokes they told and the insults they called customers behind their backs, he didn't think it was his coworkers' either. But there they were, standing at the back of the van, naked as jaybirds.

None of them were even bothering to attempt to cover themselves either. Kel looked serious as hell, but Matt had a smirk on his face. Although why, Graig couldn't imagine. He certainly had nothing to brag about, having the smallest dick in the bunch. Ray was even semihard, a fact that made Graig turn his head as he blushed. What the fuck was going on?

And why was Brandon just smoking his cigarette, completely clothed?

Myles, clad only in his basketball shorts, slid on his rump along the floor of the van until he got to the back doors, and then hopped out. The shorts quickly came off, and Graig tried not to gawk. Even limp the little guy was a good five inches. What the hell was it like when he got excited? No wonder Myles was so popular with the ladies!

Graig looked at Brandon, standing there so calm, cool, and collected. "Hey, man, I gotta tell you. I'm not really feeling too comfortable about this... whatever it is."

Brandon grinned. "And you don't even know what it is yet. Wait a second. Kel, why don't you show him?"

"Sure thing, boss," Kel said as he stared at Graig.

Graig wasn't sure what to expect, but he certainly wasn't ready for what he saw. Kel's spiky brown hair seemed to be getting longer as Graig watched, and hair—no, *fur*—was sprouting on his cheeks and chin. Graig blinked, sure his eyes were playing tricks on him.

No, Kel was changing. The bones under his skin seemed to be moving, and Graig could hear the cracks and pops as they shifted. Kel's face contorted, and he doubled over, crying out in pain. His legs were now covered with thick brown hair, and his feet were changing more than anything else. His heels were lifting off the ground, forcing Kel to stand on just the balls of his feet.

Like they were paws.

And his hands. His nails grew into claws, sharp and dangerous. Kel's mouth seemed to grow, and his teeth were now bigger, jagged like a shark.

No, a wolf.

For that's what Kelvin Hicks was now. A wolf. Kel was a werewolf. If Graig hadn't seen the transformation with his own eyes, he wouldn't believe it.

The process complete, Kel—or what had been Kel—turned and ran off into the darkness.

"Okay, guys," Brandon said as he began to pull off his shirt, "have at it."

And just as Kel had, the others changed. Slowly they became wolves. Each was slightly bigger than they were as humans and retained, in a weird way, their own hair coloring. Myles as a wolf was nearly blond, while Ray was now a dark-haired beast, running off and howling into the night. Matt, like Kel, was a gorgeous brown.

The four wolves quickly disappeared down the road, out of Graig's sight. It wasn't until they were gone that Graig realized he was holding his breath. Feeling light-headed, he turned to Brandon.

Brandon, cigarette still dangling from his lips, was standing on one leg to get the rest of the way out of his jeans. "If you don't take off your clothes first," he explained, "they're goners. Even if they don't split during the transformation, they'll be tatters by the end of the night."

"What the fuck is going on?" Graig couldn't care less his voice came out as a squeal.

"Need you to come out of the van. Then I'll explain."

It was the last thing Graig wanted to do. He wasn't even *sure* he could, as he was shaking so much from fear he was positive his muscles wouldn't respond. Hell, it was a miracle he wasn't screaming and crying like a baby. Shock. He was in shock.

Did shock make you hallucinate? No, it was seeing the guys turn into animals that had put him in this state. And he *had* seen it.

Come out of the van? Graig wanted to curl up in the back in a fetal position until he was rescued by sane, normal people.

Brandon tossed his cigarette onto the ground and let it smolder in the grass. He was wearing briefs with the Superman logo on them, and Graig might have found that humorous under other circumstances. The only other thing he had on was a leather bracelet, a thick, bulky-looking thing on his left wrist. At first Graig thought it might be a watch with a ridiculous band, but a second glance told him it was just a bracelet. A thick one.

"I'm not going to ask you again. Come out or I'll let the boys have some fun with your carcass."

Graig knew he was whimpering as he slid out of the van, tears now streaming down his cheeks. "Don't hurt me," he begged.

Smiling, Brandon replied, "Of course I'm going to hurt you. But the pain won't last long. And then the true adventure begins."

In seconds Brandon changed. Not only did he become an animal, but he grew. So much larger than any of the other guys were. The Superman undies tore away as Brandon transformed into a hairy beast, all claws and fur and slobbering mouth.

Before he could move or even cry out, the beast clamped its jaws onto Graig's shoulder and bit down. Graig was stunned by how much it hurt. He could feel the blood—his blood—running down his arm. He could feel the sharp teeth digging into his flesh. Finally he screamed, just as the beast released him.

The last thing he saw before he passed out was the moon hanging in the night sky. It seemed to have taken on a reddish tint tonight, like it was engorged with blood.

CHAPTER 15

"AFTER THAT," Graig continued, sounding miserable, "I changed. And I'm not just talking about the werewolf thing either. My personality changed. I guess... I don't know... the power went to my head. I began seeing people, even people close to me, as insignificant. Like they didn't matter. All that mattered were the guys from Smitty's and the nights we spent together roaming the countryside."

I nodded to encourage him to go on.

"I stopped seeing Laura."

She squeezed his hand and gave him what I suspect was meant as a loving look, but she was too stunned still for her face to show much emotion. After all, she not only had to cope with the news her boyfriend was a shapeshifter, but also that his buds wanted him dead now. Robbie's driving probably didn't help.

I wondered if she was letting it all sink in or if she had just shut down her brain and was working on automatic. Her eyes had the dull glaze of someone who had given up on coping with the situation.

"It's okay, baby," she whispered.

Graig went on as if she hadn't said anything. "I didn't see any of my other friends either. Just the guys, the pack. We only went out about once a week. As a pack, I mean. Usually Saturday nights. We'd go out to some place out in the country and we'd change, then roam the rest of the night."

"Do you remember the nights as a wolf?" I asked. Not all lycanthropes did. Some blacked out and woke up with no knowledge of what they did as a werewolf.

"Only in a vague way. The feeling of power stayed with me, and I'd recall some things. One night Kel and I gutted a cow. Poor thing must have gotten lost from the herd and was just out on its own, pretty far from the nearest farm. I can still remember the terror in its eyes and how it felt to rip apart its flesh. I felt kind of bad the next morning, but... that didn't stop me. I know I've killed quite a few animals since...."

Gina's living room seemed very still and quiet. Even Emma didn't make a peep during Graig's story, although I could feel her lurking in the wall behind the couch he and Laura were on.

"So what changed?" I asked. When Graig looked at me questioningly, I elaborated. "Something must have happened to put you out of favor with your little gang. Otherwise you wouldn't be here."

Graig took his hand away from Laura and sat dejectedly with his hands in his lap. "Matt had been kicked out of his place and went to live with his folks for a few days. He and his dad had a big blowup over something. I'm not even sure what. Matt came into work one day just mad as hell, cussing and throwing stuff around. He even said he'd make sure his dad paid for what he'd said. I thought he was just, you know, letting off steam. But the other night he and Ray...."

We all knew what Matt and Ray had done.

No one said anything for nearly a minute. Laura continued petting Daisy. The clock on the wall, which had the witches from *Wicked* emblazoned on its face, seemed preternaturally loud. Finally Gina broke the silence.

"What do you want to do now, Graig?"

He blinked at her. "I don't know. I guess I got to run away. If I stay here in town, the guys will find me eventually."

Laura grabbed his hand again. "But where would you go? Do you have any money saved? I've got a little I can give you...."

"I got enough," Graig insisted. His tone changed subtly. There was just an undercurrent of anger that suddenly ripped through him. Hard to keep the wolf at bay, Graig, buddy.

"Can you always control when you change?" I asked.

Graig sadly shook his head. "I thought I could. At first, anyway. I had to will it to happen. But, well, during the cycle of the full moon, the pull is too strong. I changed one night while I was coming home from work. The guys didn't warn me about that. How I got through that night with no one seeing me was a miracle. Spent most of the time in a park, I'm pretty sure. I don't think I killed anyone." Tears came to his eyes again. "I'm sure I didn't."

I'm not sure if he was trying to convince me or himself.

Gina stood and walked over to the couch and put a hand on Graig's shoulder. "My question was more practical, actually. What do you want to do? Do you want to continue being a lycanthrope?"

"I...." Graig lowered his face and stared at his own abdomen. He wanted to do the right thing and say no, but power was like a drug.

"I can take that pain away, if you'll let me," Gina said.

He glanced up into her eyes. "No one can do that."

She smiled. "Try me."

For a second there was just a glimmer of hope in his eyes. I hated to ruin the moment, but I needed more info. "What about that bracelet Brandon wears?" I'd noticed it too, that night outside of Smitty's. I just didn't really think about it. It now sounded important.

Graig frowned. "It was a stupid leather strap. Big and chunky. Like something a biker would wear. I've never seen anything like it, really. It's kind of padded. I think there's like fur or something on the inside. You know, on the part that covers his wrist."

I was betting it was a wolf pelt. Gina and I exchanged looks, reaching the same conclusion. The bracelet was, I was sure, a talisman provided by his girlfriend, Ashley. Our rival witch gave Brandon a magic charm to make him Superwolf.

"Another thing," I said. "Where's Brandon Lewis now?"

"I don't know," Graig answered, shaking his head. "Probably looking for me."

"I meant where is he staying. He's not at his house, and the auto shop is shut up."

"Oh. He and the guys are probably crashing at Ashley's. That's his girlfriend."

"And do you have an address for Ashley?"
He did.

"So WHAT did he decide?" Nick asked.

I was driving out to Clarks Hill with Nick and Casey. It was afternoon and the weather threatened to get nasty at some point. The sky was dark and the clouds didn't look happy, mimicking my mood perfectly. The traffic wasn't bad, but we were trapped behind a guy in a battered pickup, and he was obviously afraid if he actually went the speed limit, his vehicle would fall apart, making me curse him and his offspring every mile or so. Every time I tried to pass him, oncoming cars made me rethink my options. I settled back and glowered at his license plate.

I brought Nick along on this excursion as a token of apology, really. That night we planned on raiding Ashley Campbell's little dwelling and shooting up some werewolves, and I didn't want Nick included. Much too dangerous for him. I didn't really want Robbie involved, to be honest, but I couldn't think of a good excuse to keep him out of it. Not one he'd swallow, anyway. I asked Nick to bring Casey for two reasons. One, if he and Nick were going to be a couple, I wanted to spend more time with him. And two, I might just have a use for his mind-reading powers.

I was so intent on the guy in the truck I'd forgotten what we were talking about. "Who?" I asked.

"Graig. What did he decide?"

"Oh, that. We left him and his gal with Gina. She's going to work her mojo on him. Wash the wolf away or whatever she does. By now he's totally one hundred percent human."

"Why are you waiting until tonight?" Casey asked. He was in the backseat, leaning forward to include himself in our chat. "You know where they are. Even if you don't want the police involved, wouldn't it be better to go there during the day, when they're not, you know, wolves?"

"We think because of the amulet that Brandon wears, he can change any fricking time he wants. So we'd still have that. The others, according to what Graig told us, can only change at night."

"Yeah, that's what I mean." Casey draped one arm over the passenger seat so his hand dangled over Nick's shoulder. "They're human during the day and surely much easier to handle."

I looked at him briefly in the rearview mirror. "You think they're going to listen to reason? 'Hey, guys, I know you're werewolves and all that, but it really isn't very nice. I mean, killing people and stuff. Cut it out, okay?' No, they'd object, I think. And then we'd have angry young men who, according to Graig, aren't averse to using firearms, plus a Superwolf and a witch to deal with."

"So? One look at that gun you've got in your holster, and I think they'd listen."

I did the sour face thing. "Yeah. But things would get out of hand, and I may have to shoot one of them. And I have a rule about killing humans. Won't do it if I can help it."

"But Nick tells me you're a crack shot."

I wasn't about to argue that fact. I was good, but there were too many variables.

"Someone moves just at the wrong second, and—oops—you shoot them in the head when you were aiming for their shoulder. And these are very young men, almost kids. I'm willing to bet they've all killed. Matt Elliot and Ray Smith aren't alone in the homicide department. A homeless guy here. Some poor slob out for a late stroll there. They don't leave a trace, probably throwing the remains into the river or burying them somewhere isolated, but werewolves are basically hunters. Even Graig isn't positive he hasn't killed someone.

"I haven't checked past newspaper stories, but I bet somewhere in the months since this all started, there's been a story about a gruesome murder, some guy torn to pieces. I should have asked Carson when I saw him last, but my mind was on all the blood in the room. No, best to give them the chance to change and then shoot them with Gina's special bullets."

"And then what?" Nick asked.

"Then give them over to Carson, or at least let him know where to find them. Let him figure out if he can hang a murder charge on them. At least they won't be werewolves anymore."

"What about this witch you were telling us about? The one they're staying with?"

"Gina will take care of her. Apparently they've got an old score to settle, anyway."

We turned off onto Highway 52, and I was glad to say good-bye to the guy with the languorous truck. A couple of raindrops started to spatter against the windshield. Not enough yet to give the wipers a workout.

"Seems like you're heading into a very dangerous situation," Casey said. "I mean, it's you, Robbie, and Gina against—what—four werewolves and a witch." He rolled his eyes. "I can't believe I just said that sentence. Anyway, it sounds like the odds are not in your favor, even with silver bullets and charms, which you say may not work any longer."

"We've got an ace in the hole," I told him. "A demon I call Elton is going to help us out. He owes me a favor."

Nick didn't bother to hide the shock on his face. "You didn't tell me anything about a demon!"

"Must have slipped my mind."

I wasn't making Nick feel any better. "What kind of a demon?"

"A nice one."

"I wasn't aware that there were any. The name, you know, demon, kind of denotes something nasty."

"Okay, he's not totally nice, but he's trying to be." How to explain Elton in fifty words or less? "Yeah, he's a demon, but he sort of wants to become human. Deep inside that rough, gruff exterior, there's a heart. Somewhere. I think." I concluded I wasn't doing too well, so I added, "He had a pet rat."

Nick grunted. "Oh joy."

"The thing is with him we stand a chance. Without him not so much."

Nick rubbed his forehead as if he were getting a headache. "Are you sure you don't want me to help out? Really, just say the word—"

"That goes for me too," Casey said.

"Are you guys crazy? Against a witch and a bunch of wolfies? No, thanks! Did I mention that when he changes, Brandon makes the Incredible Hulk look like a munchkin? I can't be worried about you and shoot up a bunch of werewolves at the same time."

"I'm just saying—" Nick began.

"And I'm saying no."

"Robbie's human now. He can be hurt just as much as we can."

"Yeah, and don't think I'm happy about him coming along. But I'm stuck with him. He's got leverage. He can withhold sex if I don't let him go." Not that he would, but he'd pout, and that was almost as bad.

The conversation lagged for a while. I turned off Highway 52 and onto State Road 28. Shortly after that we hit S 975 E. We were almost into the town before anyone spoke again, and it was Casey who muttered from the backseat, "Talk about out in the middle of nowhere."

He wasn't lying. The town was even smaller than I imagined. We drove down the main street, passing the school and several shops. It looked like Mayberry from *The Andy Griffith Show.* We drove through the town and found West Street per Graig's instructions, and I turned left. We saw lots and lots of cornfields and a few cows that were getting wet from the rain. Figuring we were approaching Ashley Campbell's house, I donned my disguise.

I used the Robbie Church camouflage philosophy and donned dark glasses and a baseball cap. I wasn't expecting to see any of the clan outside, especially as the weather finally made up its mind and the sky was now full of rain. Ahead on the right was a big green farmhouse. I slowed down.

Nick looked at the place as we approached. "Is that it?"

"Yep." I craned my neck to get a good view. There were probably plenty of rooms. Two floors, a basement, and an attic. The best thing, from our point of view, was that it was far enough away from town that no one was likely to hear any gunfire.

"Casey," I said, "can you do something for me? Reach out with that wonderful mind of yours and see if you can pick up any thoughts from inside there. Can you make it a one-way transmission, so to speak? I don't want anyone to know we're out here."

Casey frowned. "I can try, but I don't often come across people I can read clearly. You're one of the exceptions."

"I'm betting there's someone in there broadcasting their thoughts pretty loudly." Gina thought Casey would hear Ashley's thoughts without too much difficulty, as witches had different brain waves than humans. It was worth a shot, anyway, and it was the reason I wanted Casey to come along.

I slowed down even more as we passed the house and saw Casey in the rearview mirror, closing his eyes. He almost looked like he was in pain.

"Wow," he said. "I'm getting someone pretty damn clear. A woman."

Bingo.

"She's talking with someone. A guy." Casey shook his head and smiled slightly. "Part of her brain is thinking about how good he is in bed. Apparently he's quite a firecracker."

"Yeah," I said, "but interesting as that info is, it really doesn't help us much. Can you rummage around in her thoughts and see if she's thinking about a certain charismatic private detective and what he might be planning?"

Casey's frown deepened. "She's thinking about Gina. She's looking forward to destroying her."

"Anything else?"

"She's saying something to the guy, Brandon. Something about how things are going to be changing soon. Her exact words are that they're going to emerge from the shadows." Casey paused and let out some air.

"I can almost see them. In my head, I mean. I'm getting the picture. This woman and man are upstairs, in a bed. They've just finished… well, you know. They're both naked."

Casey was certainly connecting. "What else? Can you pick up on anyone else in the house?"

He shook his head. "I can hear a television, but it's faint. Sounds like they're playing video games. I just heard some guy yelling something like 'Take that!' And laughter. They're having a good time. Ashley is smiling and stroking the guy's chest."

"Lovely," I said.

"She's not worried about you."

I glanced back again. Casey was biting his lip.

"Her exact words are 'They can use their charms all they want. They won't work any longer. I put a stop to that.'"

Disappointing but hardly unexpected. "Anything else?"

"I guess this Brandon guy *is* worried about you. Saying you're unpredictable."

That was true, but I wondered how he knew.

"And she's reassuring him, saying she's taken care of you already," Casey continued. "She's got a plan for you in place. The only person they have to worry about is the witch, she says." He grunted in pain and his voice became strained. He was wincing, his eyes tight shut. "I think she knows someone is reading her thoughts!"

"Okay, shut it down. Quick!" I flashed another look back to see he had opened his eyes. I figured that meant he'd cut off the link, so I pressed my foot hard on the accelerator.

I wanted to get us out of Dodge as quickly as possible. Well, Clarks Hill, anyway.

I slowed down once the house was no longer in sight. Nick was biting a fingernail. "What did that mean, she's already taken care of you? How? You're right here. Nothing has happened to you."

"I don't know what it means," I said, "but something tells me I'm going to find out."

CHAPTER 16

ROBBIE, GINA, and I were in my apartment, planning strategy. Gina and Robbie were on the couch, Daisy between them. I was pacing, as sitting just wasn't possible.

Gina left Graig and Laura in the extremely safe confines of her apartment. Emma at first grumbled over having houseguests, but soon was acting as a sort of unseen host, humming tunes to cheer them up, changing channels on the TV for them so they wouldn't have to pick up the remote, and generally making a nuisance of herself. If they even mentioned going out for any reason, Emma made the room darken and filled the air with a sense of threat, and the couple quickly changed their minds. In short Emma became a babysitter.

We decided we needed to get to Ashley's farmhouse in the early evening, just in case the boys decided tonight would be a good time to wolf out. Although considering the weather, they'd get their fur all wet and musty smelling. Of course the earlier we did this, the bigger the chance of someone driving down West Street and hearing the commotion. I figured we'd have to chance it, though.

"If they take a prowl outside, they'll be harder to find. They could get lost in the fields and woods out there, and we'd never find them."

Robbie was munching potato chips from a bowl he'd placed on the coffee table. "What I don't understand," he said, his mouth full of chips, "is how they even know there's a connection between Gina and you. It's not like you advertise that you work in connection with a healing witch."

"They've obviously done their research," I said.

"It's almost like they've planted a mole in our midst," Robbie said, half-kidding. "You know, a double agent."

That seemed to spark something in Gina's mind. "They wouldn't even have to do that. Ashley, as she calls herself, could have sent a familiar to spy on us. You haven't noticed a cat around lately, have you? One that you've seen in several places?"

"No, I—" It hit me. "Could it be a crow? A big-ass bird?"

Gina nodded.

Robbie's eyes widened. "There was that crow at the Elliot house when we went to see Carson."

"And," I said, "there was one outside the restaurant that night I met Nick and Casey for dinner. Also huge. Could have been the same bird."

"Have you seen it in other places?" Robbie asked.

"Do I look like the kind of guy who keeps tabs on crows?"

"Well," Gina said with a shrug. "We have to assume that Ashley has been keeping tabs on us. Anything we've said outdoors has probably been reported right back to her. Inside as well, if we've left a window open."

"She speaks crow?" Robbie asked.

Gina gave him a withering look. "She'd get the information telepathically."

"Have we said much while we've taken Daisy out for food?" I asked.

None of us could really remember.

"Well, shit," Robbie muttered. "No wonder they know so much about us."

"Well, we'll have to—"

My cell phone rang, so I put off telling them what we'd have to do. It was Carson's number, which probably wasn't good news. I answered. "And what can I do for you, Lieutenant?"

"You can get your ass out here pronto" was his gruff reply.

"Lonely, Lieutenant?" It wasn't the time to joke, but I couldn't help myself.

"I've got Matt Elliot with me. We got a tip and picked him up at Eagle Creek Park. We're still there, pretty close to the entrance. He says he's willing to talk, but he wants you present."

I glanced at the clock. There was still a couple hours before dark, and Eagle Creek wasn't far. I could get there and we'd still have time to get to Clarks Hill by nightfall. Barely. "Why haven't you taken him downtown?" I asked.

I thought it was a legitimate question, but Carson let out a few choice words his mother wouldn't have approved of. "Just get here. I can explain when I see you."

"Give me fifteen minutes."

"And come alone. Sorry, but he's insisting on it."

"Did he say why?"

"Just get here. Pronto," Carson said before cutting off the connection.

I stowed my phone away and smiled at Gina and Robbie. "Well, that was odd." I gave them the gist of the conversation.

"Freaky," Robbie agreed. "Carson should have hauled Matt Elliot's butt down to headquarters so fast his head would have spun. And come alone? Who says that except for the baddie in movies when the good guy is walking into a trap?"

I nodded. "It does sound like a trap."

"So you're going." Robbie didn't make it a question. He knew me too well.

"Yep. Gina, can I borrow your car?"

As she fished out her keys, she asked, "Why my car?"

"I'm betting there's a big-ass crow outside waiting for me. Maybe a different vehicle will confuse him."

"Right. That crow's probably smarter than you are. Are you sure it was Carson's voice?"

"Sounded like him."

Gina tossed the keys to me. "And you're going to go alone?" She didn't add "you idiot," but it was implied.

"Yep."

Robbie got up fast. I'm pretty sure he was planning on physically stopping me from walking out the door if it came to that. "You can't go. It's suicide."

"I'm going. And I'm going alone, as instructed." I smiled. "But as I'm taking Gina's car, I don't see why someone couldn't follow along, say in ten minutes."

It took Robbie a whole two seconds before realization dawned. "Oh," he said.

"He said just inside the main entrance. Make sure you're armed, both of you."

Gina sighed. "I'm never going to get to grade those damned papers."

I WAS right about the crow, which let me know that, indeed, I was walking into a trap. Well, that or it was just a fat crow that had taken to hanging around me, loitering near my parked car.

The good thing about *knowing* you're walking into a trap is you can be prepared. The bad thing is it's still a trap.

I'm not sure if Eagle Creek Park is the largest in the city, but it would do until a bigger one came along. It was on Fifty-Sixth Street, not horribly far from my apartment, but the drive there seemed to take forever. Maybe it was the uncertainty of what I'd find waiting for me there. I was also worried about Carson. Was he okay? Why did he make the phone call? It didn't *sound* like he'd been speaking under duress, and the cussing certainly was indicative of his usual self. Was the story actually legit, and I'd arrive to find Carson there with one or two of his cronies and a subdued Matthew Elliot? It'd be nice. I'd feel a bit like a fool, but I was used to that.

Pulling into the park, I saw no sign of Carson, Elliot, or anyone else, for that matter. Driving a little farther, I came to a bend, and there, parked along the side of the road, was a dusty green pickup truck. It was parked right in front of the little kiosk where park workers charged people an entrance fee before they allowed you to enter the park proper. Oddly the kiosk was unmanned. Standing next to the truck was a blonde woman of medium height wearing tight jeans, a Western-styled blouse, and a straw cowboy hat. I recognized her immediately as the woman in the photo with Brandon Lewis.

The hood of the pickup was raised, and she waved for me to stop and help as if she were having car trouble. My first thought was how stupid did she think I was, but then I remembered she had no clue I had a pic of her.

I pulled the car to a stop right behind the truck and got out. I had one of Gina's hex bags in my pocket, the amulet around my neck, and other goodies stashed about my person, feeling that, like the Boy Scouts, it was best to be prepared. I also had my .38 in the holster under my jacket, and I hadn't bothered to zip up so I could get to it easily. Yeah, she could see it, but I didn't care. I was sure she didn't either.

I walked over to the truck, trying to look like I was falling for her ploy. "What seems to be the trouble?"

She had amazing eyes, the color of amethysts. There was also the ghost of a smile playing about her lips. If I didn't know better, I'd guess her to be in her early twenties.

"I don't know," she said. "It just won't go."

When I came within a few feet of her, she winced and put a hand weakly up to her temple, obviously shaken by something. It could have been the hex bag, which was designed to ward off witches. When Gina made it, I had to add the last few ingredients, as she couldn't do it herself. We actually made it a long time ago, on another case we thought might involve one of her kind. We were wrong then, but luckily we kept the hex bag in storage just in case a need for it cropped up again.

"Got gas?" Hey, if Ashley Campbell could play the game, so could I.

She stepped back from me until her butt hit the side of the truck. That seemed to give her enough distance from the bag so at least now she didn't look like she was about to faint. "Of course," she said. The smile was now forced.

Just to mess with her, I came closer, and she paled and turned her head. Vomiting looked like an option. "Well," I said, "let me take a look. Maybe I can figure out what's wrong."

Ashley Campbell had had enough of the game. She muttered some words, which sounded to my ears as something like "Kabetha malefelerium," and held out her right palm. She didn't actually touch me, but I was shoved back almost a foot nonetheless.

The color came back to her cheeks. Apparently the hex bag had to be real close to work. Damn.

"Let's drop the pretense, Mr. Andrews," she said through clenched teeth.

"Fine by me," I replied. I looked around. "So what have you done with Lieutenant Carson?"

She pulled a crudely made cloth doll out of her pocket. It looked like something a third grader might have made out of scraps and string. The figure wore a crude suit and had the stub of a cigarette tied to one of its arms. I assumed the stub was one of Carson's discarded cancer sticks.

"I always told him that habit could kill him one day," I said.

"Oh," Ashley said, smiling as she turned the doll over and over in her hands, "I certainly could have killed him, but I needed him alive so I could borrow his voice. It was me who called you, Mr. Andrews. I hope I was convincing."

"Calling me a fuckhead was genius. Just the sort of thing Carson would have done." I eyed the doll doing flip-flops in her hands. "What's that doing to the lieutenant right now? Is he dancing around like a dervish?"

Ashley looked at the doll like she'd forgotten she had it. "No, I'm sure your precious Carson is just fine. His stomach might be slightly upset, but nothing more than that. I didn't know his name, by the way, so thank you for that bit of information. I just knew he was a cop who called you in when Matt and Ray got a big naughty."

"A bit naughty? They murdered three people."

"Like you murdered Myles Sprouse?"

I held my hands up. "Not guilty. That was Brandon's fault for trying to change him back. You should have told him it wouldn't work."

"Unfortunately I wasn't around to keep him from biting Myles again. The poor boy was dead before I got there." Ashley dropped the doll onto the ground. She squared her shoulders and looked at me, all business now. "You're an interesting man, Mr. Duncan Andrews. I could tell by the tone of your voice that you suspected this was a trap, yet you came anyway. Alone, as instructed."

"I was curious."

The smile once again made an appearance. "And we all know what curiosity did for the cat."

"I'm not a cat," I said as I drew the .38 out of its holster. I leveled the gun right at her forehead and pulled the trigger. Generally I didn't like to shoot anyone unless they were attacking me, but Ashley Campbell was dangerous and, after all, not human. I had different rules for nonhumans.

It didn't matter because the gun jammed.

"Oh dear," she said as she reached into her pocket again. Ashley pulled out a small hunk of metal I recognized as a spent bullet. It was dented and marred, but you could still tell it was silver. One of mine. It was embedded in some sort of clay. "I had to dig this out of the wall in Brandon's house. We looked for a bullet from your friend's gun, but we were pressed for time. We'll find another way to deal with him. Such a handsome boy. It'll almost make me sad to see the boys tear him apart."

I slammed the butt of the gun against the side of her face. It took her by surprise. Hell, it took me by surprise. Another one of my rules is not to hit women—unless they were really asking for it, like trying to kick you in the nuts or something—but I reacted to her threat against Robbie without really thinking. Besides, as previously stated, she really wasn't human, so the rules were different.

It was a good blow and nearly knocked her off her feet. Her lip was split, and there'd be a nice bruise she'd have to deal with. When she recovered and threw her head back to get her long locks out of her face, she didn't look happy. In fact, her eyes blazed with hatred.

Good one, Andrews. Get a powerful witch pissed off at you when you're alone in a deserted park. How long had it been? Certainly I hadn't been there ten minutes yet. I had time before the cavalry arrived. Oops.

The blood was running down her chin, and she tried to wipe as much of it away as she could, getting her hand stained with crimson. She stepped sideways, as if afraid I'd hit her again. Fair dues, it occurred to me.

"Boys," she snarled, "kill him!"

Out of the corner of my eye, I saw a guy step out from behind a tree. From Graig's description, I figured this was Kelvin Hicks. Off to my right, another guy showed himself, wearing red shorts and a black tank top. Ray Smith. Closer, another figure showed, shirtless to show off his tats and muscles, wearing just some black trunks, white socks, and bulky basketball shoes. Matt Elliot.

I didn't like the odds, so I made a sprint for my car. I didn't really think I'd make it, and I didn't. Just as my fingers barely grazed the door handle, I felt rough hands on my shoulders, and I was forced to spin around. It was the Elliot kid.

Your mind worked differently when you were engaged in fisticuffs, almost like things were moving at a slower pace than reality normally did. I noticed several things, such as he had the name Theresa tattooed over his left pectoral muscle and his boxer shorts were showing above his shorts. I'd like to say I noticed his fist just as it slammed into my jaw, but to be honest, his hand was just a blur.

The punch hurt and knocked me to one side. Reflexively I raised my right arm to protect my face from another blow. I was vaguely aware Ray and Kelvin had joined Matt now, and I was dragged away from my car.

I threw a few punches. Pretty sure I did, but when you had three attackers, all of whom worked out on a fairly regular basis, from the looks of them, there wasn't much you could do. I took a few face shots, not sure who from, and I knew Ray, the boxer, sank his fist into my left side several times. In short I got the shit kicked out of me.

Kelvin got behind me and pinned my arms. I struggled, but by this time, I didn't have much left in me. I knew my lip was bleeding and I had at least one cut on my forehead that was allowing blood to gush down into my eyes, which didn't help at all. Pretty sure old Ray broke my nose too. And without being able to use my arms in defense, he now had free rein.

And he used it. The first couple of punches went right to my gut, but then he decided to work on my face a bit. With a smile he hit me so hard in the jaw I was pretty sure my toes felt the impact as well. The lower half of my face went numb, which told me he'd broken some bones.

Seeing the fight had gone out of me, Ray stepped back and let Matt have a little fun. He didn't bother with his fists. He reared back, kicked out, and rammed his left foot right into my stomach.

I was close to passing out, and I was actually hoping I would. Then at least I wouldn't feel the pain.

Matt stepped back again and looked like he was taking aim. This kick connected with my chest, hard enough that it drove both me and my holder, Kel, back several inches. Kel laughed. I didn't.

I raised my head an inch or two, which was all I could manage. Blood was streaming down my face, I was broken and battered, but I had to get at least one dig in, so as Matt stepped back, a smirk on his face, and prepared to lash out again with those basketball shoes, I muttered, "Fuck you."

With my mouth in the condition it was, I'm not sure the words were audible, but I got my point across. Matt snarled and launched himself at me, aiming a kick at my face. Just in time I used my remaining strength to wrench myself slightly to one side. Kel wasn't expecting anything from me, and he'd loosened his grip just enough that I got out of the way of Matt's kick. It connected instead with Kel's chin.

As he fell, Kel released me, and I crumpled to the ground. My ears were ringing and the guys sounded like they were underwater, but I heard some cussing and shouts to finish me off. The closest to me was Matt, and he bent over me with the intention of hauling me to my feet again.

He should have kicked me while I was down. As it was he gave me the chance to reach the silver dagger I had strapped to my right leg. I didn't have much strength, but the blade was sharp. I jabbed him right in the thigh.

Matt let out a yelp and stumbled backward. Out of the corner of my eye, I could see Kelvin was still recovering from the kick to his face, but Ray was rushing up. He feinted, making it look like he was going to kick at my face. I slashed the knife at him, but he bounced back on his heels. Recovering quickly, he kicked the dagger out of my hand.

He kicked as well as he punched. My hand spasmed, and I couldn't feel my fingers any longer as I fell back. Ray and Kel picked me up by, grasping my collar firmly. Ray held me close to his face.

"I'm going to really fuck you up now," he growled.

At least Matt was out of it. He was clutching his leg and crying, his face pale and clammy. Gina did her mojo on the blade, and the cure was coursing through his veins. We weren't sure if it would work in their human state. Now we had an answer.

Ray punched me again, his fist connecting with my cheek. I was just starting to think maybe death would be preferable to more pounding when a freak windstorm seemed to suddenly come up. The air howled, and I could see most of the force seemed to be directed at Kel and Ray. Their hair, short as it was, was blown back by the gusts.

"Now," said a familiar voice, "you've pissed me off."

Kel had taken over holding me erect, and he let me go. My legs weren't up to the task of me standing on my own, so down I went. The world seemed to spin. I saw Ashley, still by her truck, a look of shock on her face. Once down on the ground, I shifted my head slightly so I could see the reason for her consternation.

Coming down the road was Gina. She had her hands held out in front of her, and they were glowing with energy. Her long black hair was flying back, as if the wind she was creating was originating from her skull, which for all I knew, it was.

Kel, still caught in the maelstrom, took a step forward. It took a lot of effort. "Bitch," he growled.

With a flick of her right hand, Gina sent Kelvin flying. He was literally airborne for a second and came down hard at the base of an oak tree. He made a feeble effort to get back up but then collapsed again.

I hadn't noticed, what with being so grateful Gina finally made an appearance, but Robbie must have been right behind her, for now I could see him at her side, taking aim at Ray with his .357. Gina, seeing the boys were out of the game for now, at least, turned to Ashley. The two witches just stared at each other.

Robbie had a look of intense hatred on his face, and I was afraid he was going to fire. "Don't," I croaked.

"Why the fuck not?" Robbie asked.

"You can't," I said. There was supposed to be more, but the broken jaw was making my words difficult to get out. "Can't shoot him when he's human."

"Wanna bet?"

Ray looked terrified, which made me feel an iota better, which wasn't saying much. I had to swallow hard to get another word out. "Don't."

Robbie had both hands on the gun and repositioned his stance, aiming right at Ray's chest. "You so much as twitch and you're dead meat."

Ray took him at his word and did a credible imitation of a statue. Off to the side, Matt was still writhing and whimpering, trying to staunch the flow of blood. I was pretty sure Kelvin had passed out.

Which left Gina and Ashley. The wind emanating from Gina had died, but you could still see the energy crackling in the air around her. Ashley was wary, waiting to see if Gina would make the first move. Suddenly there was a glint in her eyes, and she muttered some unintelligible words under her breath. I couldn't tell from my vantage point, at first, why a triumphant smile was on her face. Then I saw her left foot was poised over the doll of Carson.

"One move," Ashley warned, "and Duncan's policeman friend is a dead man."

Gina froze, uncertain what to do.

"Lower your gun, pretty boy," Ashley told Robbie.

Robbie looked to me to see what he should do. I nodded. Moving my head hurt, but then every part of me was hurting, so it really didn't matter.

Robbie lowered the gun.

Ashley didn't take her eyes off Gina. "Ray, grab Kel and get him into the truck."

Old Ray was confused. "What about Matt?"

"If you can move him quickly, get him as well. Otherwise leave him. He's useless to us now, anyway."

Matt let out a loud moan, either from pain or the treachery of someone he trusted. Ray went over to Kelvin first, who had already started to stir. Ray got him to his feet and helped him over to the truck. After he was bundled inside, he checked on Matt.

Leaning over the profusely sweating young man, Ray asked, "Can you move, Matt?"

"Fuck no, I can't move!" It was hard to shout through clenched teeth, but Matt managed it.

Ray apparently was reluctant to leave a man behind, so he roughly grabbed Matt's arm and yanked him up. Matt screamed and moaned with each step, but with Ray's help, he got to the truck. Ray slammed the hood shut and got into the back. Still keeping Gina in her gaze, Ashley leaned down to pluck the doll off the ground.

"We're leaving now," she said. "Nothing will happen to your cop unless you try to follow us. I suggest you tend to your wounded instead."

Cautiously she moved around to the driver's side of the truck and got in. The engine revved and she maneuvered the vehicle around Gina's car, and then the tires spun as she pulled away.

As soon as they were out of sight, Robbie and Gina were at my side.

"That was the longest ten minutes I've ever known," I said, gritting my teeth. Something clicked in my jaw halfway through the sentence, and the last few words were more a moan that anything else.

"Sorry," Robbie said. "Traffic." He brushed his hand through my hair, as there was hardly any other spot he could touch that wouldn't make me wince. He glanced worriedly at Gina. "Can you do something for him?"

Gina put her hand on my chest. I could feel warmth spreading through my veins. It was almost like getting morphine. I still hurt, but I didn't care as much.

"Let's get him home," she said. "I can treat him better there."

With difficulty Robbie got me off the ground. With my arm around his neck and his around my back, I hobbled slowly over to Gina's car. My car, I could see now, was parked just around the bend. There was no way I'd get to it. Gingerly Robbie deposited me in the backseat. Before closing the door, he looked back in to make sure I was okay.

"You doofus," he said. "You knew she had something cooked up for you. She even said she was taking you out of the equation. Now we know what she meant." He was wearing a Disney World T-shirt, which was now stained with my blood.

"I killed your shirt," I croaked.

"You keep doing stupid shit like this, and I'm going to kill you," he said, but he was smiling a smile he didn't want to show. He slammed the door after making sure my feet were inside.

As we pulled out of Eagle Creek Park, the sun was low on the horizon and night was falling. It began to rain in earnest, and I listened to the drops hitting the car as I closed my eyes. I must have fallen asleep or passed out, because the next thing I knew, I was in bed. I was alone and pretty much covered in bandages. Outside a storm was howling.

I knew how it felt.

CHAPTER 17

ROBBIE WAS sitting in a chair next to our bed and holding my hand.

"I love you. You know that. But you're flipping bananas."

"You knew that already," I told him.

It was still Saturday night, or more precisely Sunday morning, as it was well after midnight. I felt like someone who'd been run over by a truck, or at least had the shit beaten out of them by three guys. Gina was in the other room, working on a spell or two to get me better. My wounds were bad but not horrible, at least from my point of view. Jaw broken, a possible cracked rib, and the rest were just cuts and bruises. Granted, there seemed to be a *ton* of cuts and bruises, but I've been through worse. My whole body hurt. Even my eyelids hurt. Okay, maybe that was exaggerating things a bit, but you try getting the shit kicked out of you and see how you feel.

But even as I sat propped up against the headboard, I could feel Gina's magic doing its stuff. My jaw was less painful, and I could talk without feeling the damned thing click every other word.

Robbie held my hand up to his lips and kissed my fingers.

"You're in no state to get out of bed."

"I don't have to."

"You said you needed to find out what they were up to, that you were afraid they'd pull up stakes and vamoose."

"Only one of my worries," I said. "That one, though, I've got covered. Can you hand me my cell phone?"

Robbie frowned, suspicious. "Why? Who you calling?"

"Carson. I have to make sure he's okay and that she kept her word and didn't use the doll."

Relenting, Robbie handed me my phone. I didn't bother calling Carson's office, assuming he was at home snoring or maybe fondling his wife, a mental picture I never wanted to have spring into my head again. I rang his home number, which he reluctantly gave me years before when we were working on a case involving some dead delivery boys. Turned out to be a demon who got his victims by ordering pizzas. The pizzas went uneaten.

It rang seven times and then went to his voice mail. I didn't leave a message. Instead I called the number again. If he was asleep, he might need more than seven rings to stir him. This time he answered. He didn't sound happy.

"What the hell do you need at this time of night, Andrews?"

It was nice to hear his familiar growl. "Just making sure you were still alive, Lieutenant."

That seemed to fluster him. "What? W—Alive? I... of course I'm alive, you asshole! Do you know what time it is?"

"About two unless the clock on the wall is lying to me."

I heard Carson moan. "This had better be good. Why are you calling?"

"I already told you. To make sure you're alive."

Carson got creative with his curse words before hanging up. I handed the phone to Robbie, who deposited it on top of my dresser. He resumed holding my hand.

"Seriously," he said, "what possessed you to go out there? You already knew Ashley had something in mind for you. You knew it was a trap. Why go?"

I could tell he didn't want a flip answer, so I pondered a moment before replying. "Honestly? Because I figured it was Brandon Lewis I'd be meeting. I'd rile him until he changed into a wolf, and then I'd plug him with one of Gina's bullets. That would have taken care of most of our problems. Without the pack leader, the rest of the boys would be easy to handle. I wasn't counting on meeting up with the witch, although I knew that was a possibility. Also I figured they wouldn't try anything too brazen in Eagle Creek Park. I thought there'd be more people about. Seriously, why weren't more folks there, packing up their picnics and heading out to go home and watch reality TV?"

"Maybe because it's been raining off and on all day?" Robbie suggested.

I had to concede he had a point, although I expected there to be a park worker in the kiosk. Maybe there was and Ashley "convinced" them to head on home. "True," I said. To corroborate Robbie's words, a peal of thunder rattled the window. "This case has me in a moral dilemma, you know."

"How so?"

"The guys working for Lewis, Kel and Ray and the rest… they're pawns. If it weren't for Lewis, they'd just be regular young men going about their business. They don't deserve to be, for want of a better word, hunted."

"Um, excuse me," Robbie said, "but Lewis's little crew just walloped the crap out of you. They would have killed you too after they finished torturing you. Plus two of them ripped a family to shreds." He looked out the window. Rain was pelting against the panes, and we could see a flash of lightning. "At least now we don't have to go out tonight. The weather sucks."

As we were talking, I was feeling better and better. I wouldn't say I was ready to go run a marathon, but I didn't feel like I was at death's door either. I rubbed a hand on my chin. There was a vague numbness, but everything seemed to be in working order. Gina was a marvel.

And the marvel chose that moment to come into the bedroom. She herself looked a little tired. I'm sure all the incantations she uttered in order to get me better were taking a toll. Still, even frazzled, she held herself with grace and dignity. And with every hair in place.

"And how is the patient doing?"

"Ready to roar," I replied.

She came and leaned over me, stroking my jawline. "I wouldn't be doing too much roaring for a day or so. You're still mending."

Daisy had followed Gina and hopped up onto the bed, wagging her little tail. Immediately I forgot every ache and pain in my body and scooped her up into my arms. There's nothing like a happy dog—even a dead one that's still moving around—to help you convalesce. She twisted her head so she could lick my chin.

"Are you kissing it to make it all better, Daisy?" I asked. Yeah, it was in that baby-talk voice people used with their animals. Sue me.

Robbie kissed my forehead, making the scene a regular Norman Rockwell painting, if *The Saturday Evening Post* artist were on crack. Once my chin was thoroughly wet, Daisy settled down onto my lap. Robbie rubbed my temple gently with his thumb. It was extremely relaxing, and I felt my eyelids lowering. I had to snap them open.

"Damn, I'm tired," I said.

"You should be after what you've been through," Robbie said.

"Yeah, but I can't linger here in bed all night. We've got to head out to Clarks... Hill." Boy, I was weary. The eyes were refusing to stay open.

Gina was smiling gently. "We thought you might be idiotic enough to want to keep to your schedule, so I added a little spell to make you sleep. It'll do you good, Duncan, and allow you to heal properly. The witch bitch and the werewolves will still be there tomorrow."

I tried to move, but Daisy's weight on my lap made it really hard to shift my legs. That and they felt like lead. "But they might pack up and...." What was the word I was going to finish that sentence with?

"I find that very unlikely."

I didn't. Brandon Lewis closed his shop and left his home just because I was nosing around. This group seemed like the cut and run type. "We've got to...." What the hell did we have to do?

"Sleep, Duncan," Gina said in a tone that made it sound like the only thing to do.

Robbie kissed my forehead again, and my eyes finally convinced the rest of me they should be closed.

I slept.

WHEN I awoke the sun was shining in through the window. The storm had passed. Obviously so had the night. Daisy was now at the foot of the bed, curled up and snoring. I had slept half-propped up against the headboard by pillows and was still pretty much in the same position. No one was in the room, nor were there sounds coming from the rest of the apartment.

I wiped the sleepy sand from my eyes and looked down at my dog. "Well, that was a dirty trick," I said. She didn't reply.

The clock on my nightstand told me it was just after ten. I took a deep breath and tentatively moved my jaw around. No pain.

There was a mirror over my dresser, and if I raised my body off the pillows, I could just see my reflection. I had a half dozen bandages on my face, mostly around my eyes. The split in my lip was now just a thin line, barely noticeable. There were dark circles under my eyes, but they didn't look too bad.

My chest had a wrap around it, another of Gina's little tricks. I knew it was healing my cracked rib. She was good; that wasn't in question. A little devious as well, it seemed.

Although in the light of day, I knew she and Robbie did the right thing. I'd never admit I required rest and time to heal, and I'd have forced myself to go out for a little werewolf hunt while I wasn't at my peak, putting myself and everyone else in danger. Stubborn, thy name is Duncan. And if Ashley, Brandon, and crew really did pull up stakes and leave? I'd hunt them down wherever they went. After all, I had a score to settle with them, plus a client to keep safe. Until the pack was disposed of, Graig and even Maud weren't safe. And I was sure Graig and Laura were getting cabin fever, holed up in Gina's place, even with Emma to entertain them.

My stomach made a sound loud enough to awaken Daisy from her slumbers. She didn't look pleased at the interruption. After glaring at me, she snuffled a few times and curled back up to catch a few extra Zs.

I sat and wondered which I'd rather do, get up and get some food, or follow Daisy's lead and go back to sleep?

Who was I to argue with such a smart dog?

I awoke about an hour later, and now there was commotion out in the living room. I could hear voices, Robbie's and Gina's and Nick's, and they seemed to be talking about some impetuous idiot. Nick especially seemed to find my antics annoying.

"He knew it was a trap. That's all I'm saying." His voice went up an octave from anger. "One of these days, he's going to get himself killed. If he didn't have Gina here to put him back together after he does something stupid—"

Robbie came to my rescue. Sort of. "He didn't really have much choice. He knew something was up with Lieutenant Carson, as it had been his voice on the phone. As it turned out, that witch had a doll of Lieutenant Carson. She could have killed Carson with a snap of her wrist. Duncan had to go."

"He didn't have to go alone," Nick protested.

"He didn't. He had us as backup," Gina pointed out.

There was a sneer in Nick's voice. "After you stopped to get gas!"

Robbie had this way of looking totally innocent when he knew he'd fucked up, and I knew he was doing this now.

"I had no idea the car was down to fumes! And that only held us back, what, a minute or two?"

"Hey, guys," I called out. "I'm awake, and you left the bedroom door open."

Silence came from the living room. Finally Robbie yelled back, "How you feeling, Dunc?"

"Famished. Any chance an impetuous idiot can get a bite to eat around here?"

There was. Casey went out to get donuts and returned several minutes later toting several boxes filled with every imaginable kind of sweetened, deep-fried dough. As a rule, I wasn't a huge fan of donuts, but these tasted like heaven. We sat around the kitchen table and I scarfed down, by Robbie's count, half a dozen by the time he got to his second one. Gina found some milk in the refrigerator that by some miracle hadn't turned to cottage cheese, so we had something to wash them down.

I was still a bit stiff, so I'd donned a pair of sweatpants and a loose T-shirt, as they were the easiest things to get on. After we killed the donuts, Gina came around to the back of my chair and placed her hands on my shoulders. I could feel the warmth emanating from her hands. It seeped into my muscles and bones, and soon I felt like I was a new man.

She removed her hands. "How's that?"

"If you could package that, you'd make a million."

"What, and give up teaching?" She tapped my cheek, right by one of the bandages she put on me earlier. "You can probably take those off now."

"And the jaw?" I asked, although I was pretty sure I knew the answer. It was, after all, my jaw.

"Good as new. Better." She resumed her seat and nibbled at a donut. She was still on her first, and there was still half of it left. "Besides, keeping you healthy keeps me busy enough."

I had the feeling before too long we might be taxing Gina's healing powers. Even with Elton helping out, we were in for a huge battle, and I didn't like our odds.

As if reading my mind, Nick waited until there was a break in the small talk to take the floor, literally and figuratively as he stood up to make his announcement. "Duncan, Casey and I would like to offer our services."

I frowned. "I'm not sure how a history teacher and a—"

"Before you come back with a witty retort, I want to say that we've thought this over carefully, and we're making a serious proposal."

It was hard not to give in to your gut instinct. "Not a chance," I said. Even as I said it, though, I knew I should listen to him. Robbie and Gina both gave me looks that said pretty much the same thing: Hear him out.

"I think we can help. Casey certainly can since he can tap into Ashley Campbell's mind. We'll know what she's thinking at any given moment, so she won't be able to throw any surprises our way."

That was true. "And how about you?" I asked.

That momentarily flummoxed him. "Moral support?" he said with a shrug.

I was torn. On the one hand, I would be putting Nick and his new boyfriend in an extremely dangerous situation, one they might not get out of unscathed. But we had a better chance of success with more people on the team.

"Okay," I said reluctantly. "But if you get killed…."

When it became obvious I wasn't going to finish the sentence, Nick asked, "What?"

I was going to say don't come back to haunt me, but as I knew that was a distinct possibility, it seemed ridiculous to actually say it. So I said, "Just don't."

CHAPTER 18

WE WERE in a woods out east of the city, Robbie, Nick, Casey, and me. We were shooting beer cans. Well, that was the idea, anyway. The beer cans weren't in much danger, especially from Nick. The cans were perched on the top rail of a decrepit old wooden fence that was in danger of crumbling before Nick tagged one. So far he'd managed to send most of his shots out somewhere into the field behind the fence. Once he hit the fence itself, which was close but no cigar. Another time he shot an innocent tree that was a good ten feet away from any of the beer cans. Robbie stated that Nick must really have hated that tree.

Nick adjusted his ear muffs, which I'd provided, for the hundredth time and raised my spare .38 once more and aimed at an Old Milwaukee can. He pulled the trigger. The beer can remained unharmed. "I really don't like guns," he said, lowering his weapon.

"You're not going with us unless you're armed," I insisted. "In case I haven't impressed this fact upon you, what we're doing is dangerous. The wolflings will be bad enough, but Lewis is going to be especially tricky. I've seen him, and he's fast. Real fast. Like slicing your throat open before you even see it coming fast. So try again."

He did. Old Milwaukee stayed put.

Nick shook his head in despair. "I just can't seem to—"

I went up to stand slightly behind him. "You're tensing up too much. It's making your arms shake. Try this." I moved his legs a little farther apart. Then I helped him hold his arms out steady. "Look down the barrel. Don't think about it being a gun. Think of it as an extension of your arm. Breathe in. Breathe out. Then squeeze the trigger."

He missed again.

"See that old barn out in the distance?" he asked me. When I nodded, he added, "Why don't we go up there and see if I can hit its broad side?"

"You're getting better," I said. Which was true. The tree was no longer in danger. "One more time."

With a smile that showed he didn't hold out much hope, Nick took aim. This time the beer can disappeared off the fence as the bullet found its mark. I think we were all a little surprised, but Nick was positively shocked.

"Did you see that?" he said, his eyes wide. "I actually hit it."

"You did. And just think. Werewolves are a hell of a lot bigger than beer cans."

They were also faster and a hell of a lot more deadly, but I didn't want to spoil Nick's moment by pointing this out.

WE KILLED quite a few cans over the next hour or so. Casey got to be an okay shot, Nick managed to destroy one more can, and Robbie got used to the Magnum. It was as good as we were going to get in the time allowed. I just hoped it was good enough and that we wouldn't all be slaughtered before the night was over.

Robbie drove on our way back to the city, so I was free to answer when my cell phone rang. It was Lieutenant Carson.

"You bothered me last night," he said, "so I'm ruining your Sunday afternoon. How soon can you be at Broad Ripple Park?"

"I'm not in the city presently, so it might take a while. Why?"

"I've got another body. Like the Elliot family, this guy's been ripped to shreds."

Damn. "I'll be there as soon as I can."

"I'm by the entrance to the dog park. We've got the area cordoned off, but my men know to let you in."

I thanked the lieutenant and rang off. Robbie flashed a worried look at me.

"Trouble?" he asked.

I nodded. "I'm guessing the boys had a little fun after beating the crap out of me last night. Some guy in Broad Ripple is now deader than a doornail."

We didn't talk much the rest of the drive.

ROBBIE DROPPED me off at the park so he could take Casey and Nick home. I didn't think Carson would appreciate me showing up with an entourage. The entrance to the park was closed off, with two patrol cars blocking the way and two uniformed policemen stationed there just in case someone didn't get the hint. One of them examined my ID carefully before letting me through. He pointed to where I was supposed to go, which wasn't necessary, as there was an army of police officers roaming around the large fenced-off area designated as the dog park.

Carson was standing over the body, chatting with someone I gathered was from the medical examiner's office. When he spotted me, Carson waved me over.

It looked like the guy had run across the parking lot trying to get away from something chasing him. At a guess I'd say he tried to scale the fence around the dog park and didn't make it. It didn't matter. He was toast as soon as the werewolves spotted him.

"We haven't ID'd him yet," Carson told me, not bothering to introduce me to his friend. "My guess is he was doing some late-night jogging and something jumped him."

"Something," the guy next to him said, shaking his head.

I looked down at the body, or what was left of it, which wasn't much. One arm was gone entirely, and the rest was a mess. They sliced the poor guy so much you could see his ribs. There was a bunch of black hair atop a face that was whittled down to the point where it was unrecognizable. There wasn't even a nose left. The guy was wearing jogging clothes. There wasn't much left of his shirt, save the collar and a few blood-soaked strips. Oddly his dark-blue shorts were nearly intact. He was gutted, and his innards were now outards. It wasn't pleasant, and I didn't let my eyes linger too long.

"When was he found?" I asked Carson.

Carson didn't answer right away. Instead he said to his companion, "You guys can have him now. Take him away."

"Oh, joy," the guy replied.

Carson walked away from the body, obviously expecting me to follow along. I did. The lieutenant looked more tired than I'd ever seen him, and that was saying quite a lot. He rubbed a hand across his chin, feeling the stubble. He walked up to one of the patrol cars in the parking lot and then stopped, staring up at the sky. "Body was found just about three hours ago. Guy was bringing his dog to the park and got quite a little surprise. Dog wasn't real happy about it either."

I frowned. "He can't have been lying there all morning. Surely someone would have—"

"He wasn't. Our witness was busy parking, and the dog was excited for his day in the park, so the guy didn't pay a lot of attention, but he says there was a van parked close by. He says two young men were dumping something out of the back, but he didn't see what it was. Had no idea until he parked and got his dog ready. By then the van had pulled away and the guy saw what they'd unloaded."

"Did he get a good look at the guys?"

"Not really. He's downtown right now, and we're hoping we can get more out of him. All he could tell me was that they were white and looked like punks. One was shirtless and had a few tats. All wore ball caps. Maybe the sketch artist can get something to go on, but I don't know." Carson sighed deeply, and his shoulders slumped like they had the weight of the world on them. "This was your werewolf again, wasn't it?"

There didn't seem any point in hiding anything from him. "Yep. Although it was likely more than one."

He shook his head and then looked at me in surprise. I guess it was the first time he really took notice of my appearance since I arrived. I was able to ditch the bandages, but my face was still bruised, and I still wore the wrap that was healing my ribs.

"What the hell happened to you?"

"I ran into the guys who did this early last night. We got into a bit of a tussle."

The weariness seemed to melt away from his face, and Carson glared at me angrily. "You can ID these assholes?"

"If I did, Dave, what good would it do? Yeah, you could haul them in for questioning, even put them in a cell overnight. As soon as night fell, however, they'd change, and half the police force would be dead."

He was so mad he didn't even notice my use of his first name. "I can't just sit back and let them—"

"I said I'd take care of it, and I will. I was going to last night, but I got slightly beat up."

"Slightly!" he snorted.

He should have seen me before Gina worked her magic. "Thing is, Lieutenant, I know who they are. I know where they are. And I'm going to take care of it. I promise."

Carson rolled his eyes. "You and what army?"

"I've got one, strangely enough." I looked around to make sure we couldn't be overheard. A uniformed cop was heading back to his car to get something, but he wasn't paying attention to us, even though Carson's voice was getting pretty loud. At least I hoped he wasn't paying attention. Just in case, I waited until he got into his car and started rummaging around before continuing.

"There were four wolves in the pack, and the pack leader. They're now down to two." I wasn't including Graig Betz, as he was now cured and he was my client's grandson. "Myles Sprouse is dead. Matthew Elliot may be now as well. If he's not he can't change any longer, so he's out of it. So we have Ray Smith and Kelvin Hicks left. Those were the two in the van. And then we have Brandon Lewis and Ashley Campbell, the ones in charge."

Carson narrowed his eyes at me. "It's not like you to be so open. Usually you hem and haw and tell me little or nothing. What's up?"

I glanced around, mainly to make sure no cops were within earshot, but then I noticed a bird or two in the area. One, a robin, was hopping along the grass near us, probably scoping the ground for a juicy worm or something. Atop a post of the fence surrounding the dog park was a crow. And there were likely dozens of birds in the trees off in the distance.

"Let's continue this chat in your car, if you don't mind," I said. "I don't want the birds to overhear."

Blinking, Carson said, "For a moment there, I thought you said you didn't want the birds to overhear." When I didn't correct him, his eyes took on that look people get when they think they need to hide the sharp objects from you. "Holy shit, you're serious."

"Never more so. Shall we go?"

Not another word was spoken until we were safely in the confines of Carson's car. On the way I contemplated giving the middle finger to the crow but refrained in case it was just an innocent bird. That, and I worried what Carson's men would think if I flipped the bird to a bird.

In the car I gave it all to Carson. Every detail. I started with Maud Betz as my client, took him through my first meeting with Brandon Lewis and everything that happened since. A couple of times during the tale he looked like he wanted to interrupt me, but then the question died on his lips. When I got to the crow bit, he stared at the bird on the fence, which hadn't moved. In fact, it seemed to be watching my car. It may have been my imagination, but I was pretty sure Carson shivered, especially when I told him about the doll with his cigarette attached.

He sat quietly for nearly a minute after I finished. I let him gather his thoughts. Finally he spoke.

"A witch. One who can spy on you via birds. And one who had a voodoo doll of me."

"Yeah. Didn't really look like you, but it worked." I reached into my pocket and took out a charm Gina made for him. "Wear this. Don't take it off even when you shower."

Did his fingers tremble a little as he hooked the talisman around his neck? "This is out of my depth," he said.

"Now you see why I don't tell you things like this, and why I deal with them on my own."

"Why do you?" he asked. "Seriously for once."

"It's my job."

The charm seemed to calm him a little. He nodded at the crow, which still hadn't moved, although it now seemed to be watching the removal of the body. "So the bird goes back and reports to this witch? Is that how it works?"

"Not exactly. Part of her mind is in the bird, so she sees and hears what it does. Gina's done the same sort of thing before, although it's not her usual mode of operation."

"Gina's a witch. And you have a friend that's a demon."

"I don't know that I'd call him a friend. He owes me, though. So he'll help."

Carson shook his head and then closed his eyes. It was a bit much for him. He pinched the bridge of his nose. "I always knew there was a lot of weird stuff that you were involved in. I mean, I've seen a lot on cases with you that I couldn't explain. And I knew it was supernatural. I knew that. But werewolves and witches and vampires are beyond me."

"No vampires, in this case."

"Last year? We had several people found dead, drained of blood."

"Oh yeah. That was vampires. They're all dead now. Killed them with my little crossbow."

Carson opened his eyes. "Why now? Why are you telling me this?"

I couldn't look at him, so I glared at the bird. It flew off. Maybe it was just an ordinary crow after all, or maybe Ashley gave up on learning anything. "We're raiding Ashley Campbell's house tonight. You didn't hear that officially."

Carson snorted. "I didn't hear any of this officially."

"And I have a bad feeling about this. I don't think all of us are going to survive the night. Maybe none of us will."

He actually looked concerned. "Then don't—"

"I have to. Like I said, it's my job. We can cure the boys of the werewolf curse, although they probably don't see it as a curse. And Ashley and Brandon have to be stopped, if at all possible."

"Let me help."

I frowned at him. "I just said we're not likely to make it out unscathed. You think I'm going to let you—"

A little smile played on his lips. "I don't see as you have a choice. You're planning an illegal raid on someone's private property. An armed raid, I might add. I'm joining you, or I'll make sure my men stop you from leaving town tonight."

It's odd, but I never thought of Dave Carson as a colleague before. Yeah, he was someone I dealt with, but only because our professional careers crossed. I was seeing him in a new light now.

I looked at him. He was about the age my dad would be if he were still alive. Tall, kind of handsome, and just a little rugged. He looked like a cigarette ad from the 1960s.

And now I saw him as a very brave man.

I nodded. "We'll have to get you some silver bullets."

"Always wanted some," he replied.

CHAPTER 19

"DUNCAN, SHOULDN'T we be going?"

I was staring off into space, thinking but yet not wanting to think. My thoughts weren't pleasant. Usually my paranormal abilities were limited to knowing when there was a creepy creature around, generally one about to commit mayhem. Every once in a while, though, I got premonitions. I was getting one now, and it was filled with bloodshed.

And death.

I didn't mind so much about myself. But Robbie. I couldn't put him through dying again. Whatever it took, I vowed to keep him safe.

Hell, I wanted them all safe, but I knew in my heart that was impossible.

I looked up at Robbie as I sat in our living room. He looked so beautiful with his stupidly young face, his mop of dark hair, and his silly grin. And those eyes. He could melt the coldest heart with those eyes.

I sighed. "I don't suppose I can talk you out of going tonight?"

He snorted. "Yeah, like I'm going to miss the chance to see Carson's face when he's confronted with a werewolf."

Our plan was to take as many cars as possible, just in case hasty getaways were called for. Robbie would go with me. Carson was being picked up by Gina. Casey and Nick were, of course, going together. I had no idea how Elton was getting there, but he promised he would be. We were meeting up at a little pizza restaurant in Clarks Hill. After stuffing our faces, we'd trek out to Ashley's farmhouse on foot. A bunch of cars pulling up might give the game away.

I had the feeling, though, they knew we were coming. And they were more than ready for us.

Robbie, sensing my mood, changed his tone and sat down on the couch so he was facing me. "What's up?"

I forced a smile. "Nothing."

"And pigs can fly. You can't fool me, Dunc. Something is troubling you."

I sighed another sigh, a bigger one this time. It was accompanied by a groan. "It just seems like I'm the only person who realizes the danger we're putting ourselves in tonight. It's... it's going to be bad, Robbie. The odds are against us."

He made a "so what" face. "I'm sure," he said, "that we're all pretty much scared out of our wits. I know I am, and Nick and Casey made their nervousness known when I took them home. And Gina's trying to communicate with the Witches' Council to see if they can intervene, or so she said. And Elton... well, Elton's a demon. I don't think they get too worried about shit. If they do, they don't show it much. Carson's probably shaking in his boots, but he'd never let on."

Robbie rose from the couch and came around to the back of my chair. He put his arms around me and rested his chin on my head. "It has to be done, though. We all know that. And we'd be a lot more scared if you were doing this on your own. We've got to do what we can."

"Some of us may die," I said. What I really thought was all of us likely would, but that sounded defeatist, even to me.

"It's possible," Robbie agreed. "But we've still got to try."

"I don't think I could handle...." I didn't want to finish the sentence, so I just reached up and held his hand, rubbing my thumb against his. It was nice being able to feel his skin, the bone beneath. I didn't want to go through not being able to touch him again.

"Hey," he said, attempting cheery, "maybe we're worried for nothing. If Gina gets in touch with the Witches' Council and they get all pissy with Ashley, half our battle is over. They'll zap that bitch before she has the chance to say 'abracadabra.'"

The Witches' Council was a group of sort-of dead witches who had so much power they still could, if they so chose, use their magic to affect our world. Gina's father, Eleazar, was one of them. They were the ones who brought Robbie back to me. The trouble was, as far as I could tell, they hated to be bothered. And they needed a unanimous vote to agree to use magic here amongst the living. The Witches' Council was a cantankerous lot, and I wasn't holding out much hope in that direction.

Still, it was something. Gina could be really persuasive. If she were able to contact them.

"Out of the shadows," I muttered. "I wonder what Ashley means by that."

Robbie patted my chest. "We may never know."

I glanced at the wall clock. We'd have to book it to get to the rendezvous in time. Besides, I was getting hungry. I brought Robbie's hand to my lips and kissed each of his fingers in turn. "Let's go," I said.

"Wait!" Robbie broke away from me and dashed down the hall. He returned moments later with Daisy in his arms. "She should come with us."

"Um… why?" I wasn't opposed, not entirely. If Robbie and I didn't make it through, Daisy would have a hell of a time on her own. Gina could always look after her, provided she survived the night. And it made a sort of sense, having the whole family together in this. Still, I wanted to know if Robbie had the same idea.

"If one of the wolfies gets away, she can track them." There was a cheeky grin on his face. "No better trackers than Daisy here."

That was true. "Bring her," I said.

WE GOT to the pizza joint in Clarks Hill about an hour before nightfall. There would just be enough time to scarf down some slices before we had to head out to Ashley's. I never thought pizza might be my last meal, but what the hell.

Robbie and I were the last to arrive. The place wasn't big, and there were only a dozen or so tables in the joint, so it wasn't hard to find the gang. They had cornered two booths by the big window looking out onto White Street. Gina was seated next to Carson, and opposite them was Elton. Elton was wearing a big duffel coat and a huge slouch hat to help hide his features. Sunglasses and a scarf around his lower face helped as well, although the citizens of Clarks Hill may have wondered why this big dude was so bundled up on a fairly warm night. Nick and Casey were in the booth behind them.

Daisy was in Robbie's arms as we entered, and the waitress, a twentysomething blonde woman with bad teeth, immediately stepped forward. "I'm sorry," she said, not sounding sorry at all, "but you can't bring that animal in here. It's against the health code."

Gina raised a hand and said calmly, "They can bring the dog inside."

The waitress blinked, and then her demeanor changed entirely. She smiled at us, especially at Daisy. "Welcome to Joe's Pizza! What a lovely dog! Would you like a booth or a table?"

"We're meeting friends," Robbie said, his grin threatening to come right off his face to engulf the world. "Thanks."

We plopped down in the booth with Nick and Casey. Gina was right behind me, and she had to turn her head to greet us. "I like using the Obi-Wan Kenobi trick every now and then. It's good to keep in practice."

"Think you can get us extra pepperoni without us being charged for it?" I asked.

"Don't press your luck."

The place wasn't crowded, and the few enjoying some pizza around us didn't seem to be much interested in our tables, even though there was a huddled behemoth in a duffel coat noisily sipping a Diet Coke within their view. I wondered if that was another little trick of Gina's. "Pay no attention to the demon in the dark glasses. He's not really there." Or maybe people just really weren't very observant.

From the neighboring booth came a deep grumble. "Where the hell is the pizza?"

Gina patted Elton's clawed hand. "It's coming, big guy. We just put our order in a few minutes before Duncan and Robbie got here, and they've got to cook the damned things."

We chatted and told bad jokes and drank sodas while waiting for our food to arrive. It was obvious no one wanted to think about the task ahead of us, and the laughter, while forced, was good for our souls. The waitress brought out a large pizza and set the whole thing down in front of Elton. She grinned at everyone else. "Yours will be coming in just a second."

Elton looked up. Now I knew the waitress was mesmerized because she didn't scream. "There's more coming for me, right?"

"Yeppers. Only room on the table for one at a time, though." She smiled pleasantly at him and asked everyone if we needed refills before going back to retrieve another pizza.

While we waited I asked Gina how her houseguests were faring.

"Not too badly," she replied. "Emma is quite taken with Graig, much to the annoyance of Laura. They're getting a bad case of cabin fever and have been binge-watching *Game of Thrones*. I'm sure they'll be glad when this is all over."

Once we had all scarfed down a few slices, I thought it was acceptable to bring up business, and I asked Casey if he was getting any signals from Ashley.

He paused, a slice of pepperoni poised before his lips. Frowning, he said, "Nothing yet. I'm getting just a vague feeling that she's nearby, but she's too far away to get any thoughts."

"I guess that's a good sign," I said, not that I really knew if it was or not. Just something to say.

Robbie, a fleck of pizza sauce hanging from his lip, asked, "Can you read any of the guys? The wolfies?"

Casey shook his head. "No. Mind you, I can't read most people, at least not all of the time. I get flashes from some people, but connections like I have with Duncan, Gina, and this Ashley are rare."

From behind me Gina said, "Wait. What? Me? You can read me?" It sounded like her mouth was full.

I grinned as Casey's cheeks reddened. "Yeah. Don't worry. Your secrets are safe with me."

"They'd better be, buckaroo."

I twisted around so I could see her. "Any luck with the Witches' Council?"

She finished the mouthful of food she had before answering. "Oh yeah. Well, I was marginally successful. They're so reluctant to help out nowadays. But they did give me this."

She held up an amulet. It looked like something a ten-year-old could have made in shop class, if he had one eye shut and didn't spend too much time on it. It was vaguely round in shape and had squiggly lines converging to the center. It also looked heavy, and I was sure it could be uncomfortable to wear, as the metal still had sharp edges that stuck out and would gouge the skin.

I raised an eyebrow. "Um… it's lovely."

Gina smiled. "I think they were going for functionality over practicality." She slipped the amulet back into her pocket. "I'm only allowed to use it, though, under certain circumstances. Three conditions have to be met first."

"I'm all agog," Robbie said, mouth partially full of pizza. "What are the conditions? 'Cause if one of them is that she's a bitch, well, then one is already filled."

"First she has to demonstrate that she's a danger to the human populace at large. Second she has to take human life, and I have to see her do it." Gina paused to sip her soda.

She was about to tell us the third condition when Casey suddenly let out a cry and fell forward in his seat, nearly burying his nose in the pizza on the plate in front of him. With effort he sat back up, pinching the bridge of his nose. Maybe that helped him concentrate, or maybe it was to help relieve the headache he was getting. Casey's eyes were closed, and he seemed to be in pain.

"What is it?" Nick asked, reaching out a hand for comfort.

"She's close now," Casey said through gritted teeth. "She's here in town. Not far away, I think."

Gina asked, "Is she alone?"

I don't know if Casey even heard her. His face was contorted in agony. "Oh my God," he muttered.

"What?" I asked. "What is she thinking?"

Pinching his nose obviously wasn't cutting it, so Casey pressed fingers against both of his temples. "She's with all of them. Lewis, Smith, and Hicks. They're all there."

Something told me they weren't in town just to buy a carton of milk, especially as the witch's thoughts were causing Casey such distress. "Can you get anything more?" I asked. "We need to know as much as possible."

"Oh my God," he repeated. "They're planning…."

"What?" Robbie asked when it seemed Casey wasn't going to say anything further.

Casey opened his eyes and gazed into Robbie's face. "They're outside," he said softly. "Walking down the street toward town. She's thinking…." Casey frowned and took a deep breath. "She's… they're planning something big. A big show. That's how she sees it. A big show. They're going to show the world that supernatural creatures exist. Come from the shadows. After tonight everyone will know about her and her gang of werewolves."

Casey was now speaking in a lighter cadence, and the phrasing didn't seem to be his own, as if he were reporting to us her exact thoughts as she would express them.

"The world will know. After tonight the world will know. And people will bow to her power."

"Jesus," Nick whispered. "What are they going to do?"

Casey looked like he was about to faint from the effort of keeping a mental contact with Ashley. "In just a few minutes, when the sun goes down, the guys are going to change. And then they're going to attack."

"Who?" Robbie asked. "Us? How do they even know we're here?"

Casey shook his head slightly. "Not us. The town. They're planning on murdering almost everyone in this town, leaving only a few witnesses. They're going to kill hundreds of people, all in one night!"

Carson said a few choice cuss words as he stood. "Not if we get to them first," he said, pulling out his gun.

Gina slid across the seat so she could join him. "I'd say she's fulfilled requirement number one. Threatening the human populace."

We all got to our feet, getting our weapons ready. The other patrons of the pizza joint got very quiet, and our waitress, who was coming over to see if we needed anything more, froze midstride.

Robbie held his gun pointed to the ceiling. "And now," he said, "the battle begins."

CHAPTER 20

OUTSIDE A wind had picked up and the skies had darkened. Technically it was still daylight, as the sun had yet to set, but storm clouds converged over Clarks Hill. Despite a forecast calling for a warm, temperate evening with no precipitation, it was, at least over one small Indiana town, gloomy and dismal. Ashley, I assumed, liked to make a statement, and in her mind, a rainy night was called for.

We tumbled out into the street. Thunder cracked as I gazed down White Street to see, off in the distance, Ashley Campbell striding right down the middle of the street, her head held high. Behind her, fanned out like a flock of birds, were Brandon Lewis, Ray Smith, and Kelvin Hicks. They looked like they should be snapping their fingers and singing about what to do when you're a Jet in a bizarre production of *West Side Story*. Maybe *Gunfight at the O.K. Corral* was more apt. If I only knew we'd be reenacting that drama when I told Robbie about it, I'd have paid more attention to it myself.

There was a slight smile on Ashley's face when she spotted us coming out of the pizza joint. Our presence didn't seem to worry her, as she never even broke stride. They were still too far off to pick up the words properly, but she seemed to ask Brandon something. He nodded and replied, and his answer was a little louder, and I'm pretty sure it was "Let's do it."

I stepped out into the street. It seemed like the thing to do. Hell, it wasn't like I had to dodge traffic. Other than a drunk guy coming out of a bar down the block and a woman carrying a bag of groceries, there wasn't much going on. No cars honked, demanding we get out of the way. Apparently this was one of those towns that rolled up the sidewalks when the sun was about to dip below the horizon. On the left of us was a little community park, complete with slides and a swing set. Beyond that was the Clarks Hill Fire Department, and across the street was, unless the sign was lying, the town hall, a squat little blue-gray building that looked about as much like a town hall as I looked like Scarlett Johansson. But hey, what did I know about small towns?

No kids played on the playground. The fire station seemed deserted. And no officials were officiating at the town hall. Our only audience was a small black-and-white cat, searching for something to chase in the park. The cat, sensing something big was afoot, quickly took off. Smart cat. I wanted to join her.

The gang was behind me. I knew that without looking. Daisy was at my side, growling at the approach of Ashley and her brood. We were close to the corner of the street, and I could see a house on the side street, a little white cottage. An old guy came out, toting a garbage can, which he was intending to take down to the curb. If he knew what was brewing, he'd hold off putting out his trash.

When they came to within about thirty yards of us, Ashley stopped suddenly. She was wearing tight, tight jeans, a Western shirt, and a straw cowboy hat. The smile never left her face. The boys, perfectly in sync, ceased strutting as well. While Ashley seemed poised and cool, though, they were tense and ready to strike, especially Ray Smith. He looked like he wanted to rip into us. In a minute he probably would be.

"Well," Ashley said, tossing her head back so her blonde hair wasn't in her face, "if it isn't the private detective and his little band of misfits." She gazed over my shoulder to where Gina was standing. "And Miranda. Haven't seen you in nearly a century. My, but you've changed."

"My name is Gina now." Gina was matching her tone. We aren't worried, it seemed to say. We've got you outnumbered. True, we're one witch, a dead dog, and five human beings going against one witch, two regular werewolves, and a mega-wolf, but what the hell. "And you haven't changed much. Oh, you've gotten taller. And blonder. But you're still the same conniving bitch you always were."

Ashley's smile grew at the insult, and she turned her attention to Lieutenant Carson, who was behind me to my right. "I didn't expect to see the copper here. Come to die, Mr. Policeman?"

Carson grunted. "I'm here because I need to be. This doesn't have to erupt into bloodshed, you know."

"Oh, but bloodshed is so much fun" was her reply.

Gina, as always, tried to be soothing in her tone. "Why are you doing this, Ashley?"

Ray snorted. "Because we can!"

Ashley tilted her head skyward. Heat lightning was illuminating the clouds. "We've lived in the darkness for far too long. You of all people should know that, Miranda. It's time that people knew just what is out there in the darkness. They need to know what's moving in the shadows."

"To what end?" Gina asked. "So they can fear you?"

Ashley snapped her head forward to glare at Gina. "Yes! And they should fear me! You as well! Aren't you tired of pretending to be human? You should be standing at my side, not opposing me!" She nodded toward Elton, who'd thrown off his coat, hat, and sunglasses. He was wearing sweatpants and a large and somewhat misshapen One Direction T-shirt. If we lived through the night, I really had to learn more about our demon friend.

"And what about you, demon? Skulking in the shadows. Aren't you tired of hiding?"

Elton sniffed. "I like humans," he growled.

A snarl curled on Ashley's lips. "You're pathetic."

"They're right, though," I said. "It doesn't have to happen this way. We can talk this out. People don't have to die."

She raised an eyebrow. "So you know what we're planning? Yes, I thought I detected a mind reader in your midst. Is it you?" She looked at Nick, then Robbie. Finally she settled on Casey. "Oh yes. There you are. Even now I can feel you trying to worm your way into my thoughts. What do you see, little man?"

Casey couldn't quite keep the quiver from his voice. "I see hatred. And blood."

Ashley shook her head. "Not hatred. Retribution."

Kelvin was shifting his weight from one foot to the other, obviously anxious for a fight. "What are we waiting for? These guys can't stop us, and the sun's been down for minutes now."

Ashley, not taking her eyes off us, held up a hand to restrain him. "I want to give my old friend one last chance." She singled out Gina. "You can walk away from this. You don't have to die. You know your little charms won't protect you. I've seen to that. I'll even let you take your friends with you."

"I can't let you kill these people" was Gina's simple reply.

Nodding, Ashley said, "Very well." The smile disappeared from her face. She turned to me. "I have to know. We've been standing here for a while now, and none of you have taken out your little peashooters and fired. Why not? The boys are much easier to kill in their present form."

"We don't kill people, not unless we have to."

"I see. They're people now, and so they're protected by your code of honor. But as soon as they change to wolf form, they're monsters and therefore fit to kill."

"Only if they threaten people."

"You're a fool as well," she said. "You've missed your one chance to get through the next few minutes alive." Ashley grinned wickedly. "Go to it, boys."

With a smirk Ray began to change. Kelvin quickly followed his example. Ray cried out as his chest expanded, the dark fur spreading across his skin. Soon the tank top he wore reached the end of its stretching abilities and shredded, the tattered remains falling to the ground to be blown away by the wind. Kelvin let out a howl as his back arched, his spine twisting and grinding. The hair sprouting out of his pores was a lighter color than that of his friend.

Standing behind Ashley, Brandon's transformation took mere seconds. The tattoos on his arms were instantly covered with thick black hair, and his face and body altered in the blink of an eye. His clothes ripped away, and with a loud crack of bones, where a man was standing moments before now stood a huge, towering werewolf.

"Plan A," I said.

We rushed forward, Elton and I heading straight for Lewis. Gina had been harnessing energy since we stepped outside, and she was nearly sizzling with electric power as she came up to my right side. Robbie and Carson stepped to the right, confronting the still-changing Kelvin. Nick and Casey faced Ray, guns out and ready.

I noted out of the corner of my eye Casey was taking aim at Ray with a slightly shaking hand. Sure he was about to fire, I said, "Try to wound only! If you can!"

Casey paused, faltering, but I didn't have time to see what he chose to do. Gina had thrust a ball of energy right at Ashley, who held up a hand and deflected it. The two of them had blue fire coming off their bodies, resembling the heat lightning up in the sky. They seemed to be at a standoff, but at least Ashley couldn't do anything to protect her precious brood.

You know how, in movies and TV shows, an action sequence was often done in slow motion? In a way it made sense, not only because you got to see all the activity in detail, but because that was the way it sort of happened. Your senses were heightened, and somehow you could take in more details than you'd normally be able to do. I was running toward Brandon, Elton now ahead of me, but I was also taking in my surroundings. In a vague way, I could see Robbie and Carson converging on Kelvin, now completely a wolf. I heard Casey's shot ring out and knew, although I didn't really see the result, he'd missed. And then there was another blast from a gun somewhere behind us.

And Nick fell to the ground with a strangled cry.

Elton barreled into the big wolf that moments ago was Brandon, and they both crashed onto the blacktop of the road, snarling and trying to slash each other with their claws. I had my gun ready but couldn't take a shot without the chance of hitting Elton. A bullet whizzed by me, coming from behind, and I spun and crouched to see who shot Nick and was now trying to take me out.

Standing just down the road, a little beyond the little pizza shop, was Matthew Elliot. From what I could see, he was a completely healed Matthew Elliot. It made sense. Even though Ashley Campbell wasn't a healing witch, she still had a lot of powers. While she couldn't reverse Gina's spell and make Elliot into a werewolf again, she could at least heal his wounds to the point where he'd be able to join them in this little fracas, and she obviously had. While we were jawing with Ashley and preparing for battle, Elliot had circled around and come up behind us. The bastard. I aimed for his right arm, the one holding the gun.

He got off another shot, which made a divot in the road not more than a couple of inches from me. My aim was better than his. Well, slightly. I was aiming for his bicep and got his shoulder. The gun dropped from his hand as he fell backward.

I turned back to the combat. Nick was still on the ground, but I could see his face and I knew, although he was in agony, he was at least alive. The bullet hit his leg, and he was clutching his thigh in an attempt to staunch the blood flow. Gina and Ashley were still in their standoff, and Robbie and Carson were chasing Kelvin down a side street. Elton and the big guy were rolling back and forth, snarling, clawing, and biting. It was hard to tell who was getting the upper hand.

Casey was firing shot after shot at Ray, but the wolf had yet to be wounded. The beast had taken refuge in the little kiddie park, dodging in between the colorful slides and swings. I could tell it was toying with Casey, waiting for its moment to pounce. Daisy, however, was ensuring Smith wouldn't get away. She was running circles around the werewolf, keeping a safe distance and barking up a storm to keep Casey informed as to just where the beast was.

Unfortunately the guy who left his garbage at the curb was still standing in his drive, watching the carnage with his mouth hanging open. The wolf, close to the far end of the kiddie park, finally noticed him. Two bounds and a leap, and the beast was on the guy, who froze from fear.

He didn't suffer. Smith let out a battle roar and slashed the guy's throat before he even knew what was coming at him. The dude tried to scream, but even that was too late. A death gurgle came out of his mouth as the wolf completed the job with a few deep gashes across the man's chest. The guy was dead before he hit the ground.

Casey and I both fired. He was closer, and it was hard to say which of us hit the mark, but one obviously did. There was a streetlight close by, so I could just make out the spatter of blood and bone and brain erupting from the wound as the bullet hit him. He didn't even have time to howl. Ray fell forward, right on top of the guy he just murdered.

If he hadn't paused to revel in his kill, he wouldn't have been so easy to hit. These guys were fast, hard to get a bead on. But Ray made a mistake, and I felt a little pang of sadness it had had to end like this.

His body began to change back as he lay sprawled over his victim. In moments he'd be a naked corpse with a bullet hole in the back of his head.

I'd have paused to say something pithy, but there wasn't time. There was still Brandon, Kelvin, and Ashley to deal with.

"Take care of Nick," I told Casey.

He was staring at his gun, as if wondering how it got into his hand. He was in shock, thinking he might have just killed a person. "What?" he asked.

"He's been shot. Make sure he's all right."

I waited just long enough to see him nod and start to move. I knew he'd snap out of it as soon as he saw his new boyfriend was in pain. I whistled for Daisy, and when she joined me, we turned to see where we were needed next.

White Street was a battleground. The energy emanating from the two witches was causing cracks in the tarmac of the road, and the streetlights began to burst one by one, spraying out sparks as the bulbs shattered. Someone had come out of the pizza parlor to see what the commotion was. I think it was a middle-aged woman, but she was in the shadows, so it was hard to really tell. I just know I heard her scream and yell out something about calling the police.

On the other side of the street, near the town hall, Elton and Brandon were still fighting it out. Brandon threw Elton aside, and the demon hit the building's window, splintering the glass. There were black streaks on Elton's face. Demon blood. The wolf loomed over Elton, thinking he was ripe for the kill. Elton recovered, though, kicking out and slamming his size-sixteen boot right into the wolf's crotch.

"Fuck you," Elton growled. Then he tackled Brandon and the two went back to snarling and biting.

The woman was screeching about the police. Ashley had her right hand up, blocking Gina's energy attack, but her left hand was free, and she motioned at the woman. "I don't have time for this," she said. And the woman went up in smoke, her cry lingering in the air even after her body completely vanished. Smoke curled where she'd been standing.

Gina almost smiled. "And there goes condition number two," she said. "So, Ashley Campbell, as you are now known, I now have the authority to command you to surrender to the Witches' Council."

Ashley's determined look faltered momentarily. That worried her. "What?" she said.

"Surrender now and the council will show leniency."

I was moving, trying to see where Robbie and Carson were, but I saw Ashley square her shoulders. "You're bluffing," she said. Out of the corner of her eye, she must have seen me coming around behind her, for she flicked her left hand and a bolt of lightning flashed toward me. I jumped to my right, and the bolt hit the road, sending up chunks of tarmac.

Daisy was close at my heels but wasn't able to dodge the projectile. It didn't hit her, but the blast sent her reeling, and she got hit by a lump of broken tarmac. With a yelp she hit the ground and lay still.

I got to my feet and rushed over to her. She didn't seem to be breathing, but she actually didn't have to. Could she be dead? What could kill a zombie bulldog? I leaned down and put a hand on her side. "Daisy?" I asked, despair welling in my heart. If that woman hurt my dog, she was going to have more than Gina and the Witches' Council to worry about.

Daisy opened one bloodshot eye, and her chest rose as she began to breathe again.

"Good girl," I told her.

Shots rang out somewhere down the street. Robbie or Carson must have cornered Kelvin. I needed to help them.

"You rest," I said to Daisy. "You've done your part. We'll take care of the rest."

Hopefully.

When I rose I saw Gina's energy had expanded. In fact, the light emanating from her was almost blinding. She strode slowly toward Ashley, the amulet held before her. Ashley, a worried frown on her face, was obviously digging deep within her for more power, but it just wasn't there.

"This is your last chance," Gina said, only paces away from Ashley. "Surrender."

With a feral growl, Ashley leaped forward, trying to get her hands around Gina's throat. Gina didn't flinch but kept the amulet facing the woman. It made contact with Ashley's chest, and the witch immediately went up in flames.

Gina stood back and averted her gaze, the heat was so intense. It was like Ashley had been doused with gasoline. With a whoosh the flames engulfed her in seconds. She screamed—one of the most unholy sounds I've ever heard—and thrashed around, but there was nothing she could do. I could see her clothing burn away, her flesh crackle and blacken. The intensity of the fire was such that she was mere ashes by the time I got over to Gina's side.

Gina was sinking to the ground, and I got my arms around her just in time to keep her from falling.

"It's okay," she said. "That just took a lot of energy out of me. I'll be all right."

More shots rang out. I had to see what Robbie was up to. "Daisy's been hurt," I told Gina.

"I'll look after her." She managed a weak smile. "Go."

She knew me so well.

I ran in the direction of the shots.

I'd lost track of Elton and Brandon, but I'd have to worry about them later. I went down a side street, following the echo of gunfire. I passed several run-down houses and saw people's faces in the windows, gazing out and wondering just what the hell was going on. I wanted to tell them they didn't want to know. A loud growl came from the distance, followed by another shot.

There was a body in the street, right in the middle and covered in blood. Holding my breath, I rushed forward and knelt down. Whoever it was was lying on their stomach, and I had to shift them to their side to see their face.

Lieutenant David Carson looked back at me through slitted eyes. His face was a mess, flesh hanging off in shreds and blood everywhere. There also seemed to be a gash across his chest. But he was alive. He even managed a small smile.

"Hey," he said, his voice barely more than a whisper.

"You're going to be all right," I said. "Just keep still."

Carson shook his head slightly, and he winced. "Chest. Damn thing came out of nowhere. I think… wow. I think this is it. Never thought I'd be killed by a werewolf. Just goes to show you, huh."

"Don't talk, you asshole. You're not going to die."

"Says you. I've lost a hell of a lot of blood, and it hurts to breathe. I think this is—"

"Shut up. Gina is a healing witch. If you can just—"

"Of course she is."

I could tell Carson wanted to make a joke in his dying breath, but there was no need. If he'd just hang on.

"I bet you keep her busy."

"Actually," I said, "I do. Now it's her turn to work on you."

I don't know how she knew, but Gina knew. She came up behind me and placed a hand on my shoulder, letting me know she'd take care of things.

"Daisy's fine. She's very hurt, but she'll make it. Now move and let me see what I can do for the lieutenant."

I got out of her way, and she crouched over Carson. His eyes were glazing over.

"I think we're too late, even for a healing witch," he whispered.

"Hush," Gina said. "I'll be the one to say when it's too late."

She examined his wounds and glanced at me. I read it all in her face. It was bad. She'd do everything she could, of course. She was Gina, after all. But it was bad. She placed a hand on the lieutenant's bloody chest. A very slight green light seemed to come from her fingertips and enter Carson's wounds. Immediately his eyes cleared just a fraction.

"What the hell did you just do? Shoot me with morphine?" he asked, his voice still husky with pain.

"In a way. Now I told you to hush."

She moved her hand across Carson's chest slowly and gently, ignoring the fact she was getting his blood all over her fingers. I could see the green light travel over his skin, and as it did its work, a grin—a pained one, but a grin nonetheless—crossed Carson's face.

"Oh, she's good," he said.

Gina actually looked like she was about to faint. She was taxing her abilities to the max, and I knew she didn't have much more in her. As she switched to working her mojo on the lieutenant's ravaged face, she spoke to me over her shoulder.

"I'll take care of this. Go find the others."

I paused just long enough to give Carson an encouraging look. He nodded back at me. Then I was off.

It didn't take me long to find Robbie. There hadn't been any further gunfire, but I went in the general direction the shot had come from. He was just in the next block, standing in the middle of the road, his head bowed and his gun still in his hand. Lying at his feet was the body of Kelvin Hicks, naked and unmoving. I didn't think Robbie even heard me run up to him. When I got close, I saw tears streaming down his face.

Some of the neighbors had turned on their porch lights. The braver ones even stepped out from the relative safety of their homes and were craning their necks to get a better view. Some were on cell phones, no doubt calling the police. No one came down to check on the young man lying dead in the street.

Kelvin Hicks had reverted to human form in death, and his skin looked oddly white in the darkened street, the way tombstones almost seemed to glow in the moonlight. There was a nice-sized hole in his chest where Robbie shot him. There was some blood, but not a lot. He'd died quickly.

Robbie sniffled and I put my arm around him. He didn't shift his gaze from the body, but he knew it was me.

"I tried to wound him. I just…."

"It's okay," I told him. "You did what you had to do." I pulled him close to me, but he remained stiff and unyielding.

I tried not to pay attention to the onlookers, but it was difficult. The house closest to us had a lot of activity on the enclosed porch, but no one ventured out. Understandable, as I was sure they could see the big old Magnum at the end of Robbie's arm. Off in the distance came the sound of a siren. I wished good luck to the unlucky law enforcement official who was on duty that night.

Duncan.

My name flashed into my mind. Casey was sending me a message. *Come as quick as you can. Back to the restaurant. Hurry!*

I touched Robbie's elbow. "I'm going back to the pizza place. There's still Brandon to take care of."

Robbie nodded, and I expected him to stay where he was, but as soon as I began to retrace my footsteps, he shook himself and followed me. The first steps he took were awkward, as if his legs didn't want to respond to the commands his brain was sending out, but once he was a few yards away from the body, he was okay.

When we got back to White Street, it looked like a tornado had hit the little town. The stop sign at the corner was bent double. A car that was parked close to the pizza joint looked like someone dropped a piano on the roof and then removed the evidence, leaving just the damaged vehicle. The door to the restaurant had been torn off its hinges and tossed into the road. The window we sat by as we ate was busted out, and there was an arm on the sidewalk that had been torn off some poor soul's body. There was a mangled, bloody body in the doorway, a guy who had been eating with his family earlier. I only knew him by his clothes, as his face was unrecognizable.

Daisy was still lying in the street where she was hit, but I could see her little chest rising and falling. Her tongue was hanging out, but her eyes were open. She blinked when she recognized me and Robbie, but she was still too out of it to move.

Casey was huddled over Nick, who was at least sitting up, although he looked a sickly white from shock and loss of blood. Casey said nothing but nodded to the pizza restaurant, although the sounds of breaking glass, wood, and whatever coming from there told us that was where we needed to be.

A patrol car, red and blue lights flashing, pulled up just as Robbie and I got to the entrance to the parlor. The driver didn't bother parking but slammed on his brakes and stopped the cruiser in the middle of the street. He got out quickly, a big, chunky guy with little eyes. He took in the body in the doorway and the sounds of mayhem issuing from within. "What the hell is going on?" he demanded as he drew his gun.

Robbie and I didn't pause. What could we tell him?

Inside, the place was a shambles. Nearly every table was overturned, and most of the chairs were toppled and broken. Even the booths were destroyed. The counter where people placed their order was half-gone, the wood pieces scattered across the floor. The cash register looked like it was used to try to bash someone's head in, and the mangled remains were tossed against the wall.

The waitress who served us was slumped into a corner. Her eyes were gouged out, and she was coated in shredded clothing and blood. Her left arm was gone, ripped out of the shoulder socket. It must have been thrown out the broken window. The walls were spattered with blood.

A roar came from the kitchen, followed by a loud crash. There was a large section of the wall where you could see into the back room, but it didn't tell us much other than a fight was going on. Suddenly a huge shape burst through the doorway and nearly fell at my feet. It was Elton, and he'd been tossed with force by the werewolf. Elton didn't look good. He was covered in black demon blood, and one of his horns had been either ripped or bitten off. He hit the floor with a thud, and when he winced, I saw he'd lost a couple of his sharp, razor-like teeth.

Robbie and I aimed our weapons at the doorway, expecting the beast to emerge to continue his attack on Elton. Silence. Behind us the cop must have entered and seen the bodies.

"Oh my God," he muttered, shortly followed by the sounds of him throwing up. Elton raised his head slightly.

"Some fight, eh?" he said. "Can't… lie here all night, though." He coughed, and some blood oozed from his lips.

I listened and heard heavy breathing coming from the kitchen. The wolf was poised, waiting for us to come after him. No dummy, he wasn't about to charge out into a hail of gunfire.

Elton's fall nearly took the double doors off their hinges, and I didn't take my eyes off the entryway. I nodded slightly to Robbie. "Take care of him," I said, meaning Elton. "I'm going in."

Elton shook off Robbie's attempts to help him. "I can manage on my own," he growled. "I owe that son of a bitch."

Despite his injuries Elton got to his feet, although I could see out of the corner of my eye that he grimaced as he did so. The three of us cautiously crept up to the doorway.

Just as I got to the threshold, something knocked the gun out of my hand. The wolf was so fast I didn't even see the claws slash out, taking a deep gouge out of my thumb and sending the .38 flying. The bastard had been hiding just on the other side of the wall, waiting for any movement coming into the kitchen. I cried out, clutching my hand, as Robbie fired.

I'm pretty sure he hit Lewis in the leg, but the big behemoth barely flinched. Maybe Ashley found a way around Gina's special bullets, or maybe he was just such a huge bastard the magic didn't work immediately. Either way I was knocked off my feet as the creature came barreling out of the kitchen. Lewis slammed into me hard enough to force the air from my lungs, and I hit the wall, stunned, my vision blurring temporarily. Somehow I managed to stay on my feet, though, and I shook my head to clear things.

My eyesight came back to normal, and I wished it hadn't. Lewis charged in on all fours, but reared up once he was in the room with a loud roar. Robbie got backhanded by one of the werewolf's huge paws, and he tumbled backward, losing his footing on the broken boards from the counter. As he fell he lost his grip on the Magnum, which skittered across the floor.

Elton emitted a war cry and charged at the beast, but it had anticipated his attack and spun after knocking Robbie off his feet. The demon tried to tackle Lewis, but the wolf instead picked Elton up in a crushing grip. Elton struggled as the werewolf sank its fangs into his throat. His screams were cut short as the animal tore into the flesh, its strong jaws nearly severing his head from his shoulders.

I dove for my gun and came up firing, but it was too late. Brandon tossed Elton aside like he was no more than a rag doll, black demon blood dripping from his jaw. One shot got the beast in the shoulder, and this time Lewis seemed to feel the impact. The werewolf roared and slashed at me, but I ducked in time to avoid getting sliced to pieces. He was fast, though, and his other hand caught me on the side of the head.

I felt pain explode across the left side of my face, and I knew the claws had raked across my cheek, leaving deep, bloody gouges in the skin. I tasted blood and knew part of my lip was torn away, and maybe a bit of my ear as well. I hit the ground hard, losing my .38 again.

Robbie crawled over to retrieve his gun, but just as he got his fingers on the barrel, the werewolf pounced on him. Lewis grabbed him by the throat and spun him around to face me, effectively using Robbie as a shield so I wouldn't have a clean shot even if I could get to my gun in time. I could see the sharp claws digging into the soft skin of Robbie's throat, and that made me forget my pain and pick my gun back up. Lewis, snarling, held my lover before him, Robbie's feet unable to reach the floor.

I aimed, but the beast kept shaking Robbie, making me hesitate to pull the trigger.

The bullets Robbie and I had pumped into the werewolf were beginning to take effect. The wolf began to shrink in size, and the sound of bones shifting, cracking, and changing came to my ears. The snout was quickly becoming a mouth, and the fur was receding back into Lewis's skin.

He continued to hold Robbie before him, but in moments, he was no longer Brandon Lewis, werewolf, but just Brandon Lewis, naked and bleeding from wounds in his leg and shoulder. The only item of clothing still on him was the leather strap he had around his wrist, the one with the wolf pelt sewn into it. Strangely that hand remained a claw, poised over Robbie's neck, ready to slash the tender flesh. The strap, with its magic, was obviously powerful enough to allow Lewis's hand to remain half-wolf.

Robbie's eyes sought me out, imploring me to fire regardless of the situation. There was defiance in his face, and I knew he wanted me to take Lewis out.

The chances of hitting Robbie were too high, though. Especially now that Lewis was normal sized. I just couldn't do it.

Lewis knew it too. His face showed the pain he was feeling, but he still managed to smile. "I'm walking out of here," he said. "If you move a muscle, Pretty Boy here gets it. You got me?"

"I got you." I didn't, however, lower the gun. Why wasn't that one hand reverting back to human form? Was it because of the leather bracelet?

"He'll kill me anyway, Dunc," Robbie said, his voice strained by the grip on his throat.

"I mean it," Lewis said. "I'll rip his throat out right in front of you and you can watch your lover die, or you can let me leave." Something akin to a laugh came out of him. "You won't fire anyway, will you? You don't like to shoot humans."

Robbie strained but was still too weak from getting pummeled by the wolf to escape Lewis's clutches. He did, however, lower his face about an inch, and that's when I fired.

"That's what you think," I said.

There was an ear-deafening explosion. I didn't know who was more surprised, me or Lewis. It wasn't a conscious thought to pull the trigger, but the proof I'd done so was there in the center of Lewis's forehead, a tiny little bullet hole just below his hairline.

Mind you, if Lewis was surprised, it was only for the split second between life and death. His hands lost their grip on Robbie as he slowly sank to the floor. Robbie stumbled forward, glancing back in time to see Lewis's eyes glaze over.

Robbie came over, and we held on to each other tightly. He was shaking. I think I was too. I could have held on to him forever, but I had to check on Elton. Reluctantly I turned from Robbie and gazed down at the unmoving demon.

Robbie gulped. "Is he…?"

I didn't have to answer. We both knew. Elton's throat was nearly gone, a mess of torn flesh, sinew, muscle, and bone. The floor around his head was a black pool of blood, and his eyes, nearly the only thing on his face untouched by the werewolf's claws, stared unblinking up at the ceiling.

Standing over him, one shoe in Elton's blood, I bit my lip to fight back tears. It was odd. I really didn't know him all that well. He gave me information about Gina's boyfriend once. He had a pet rat. He strove to be more human than demon. He smoked and even dressed like he was a gangster in some old Humphrey Bogart movie. And he was a good person, or at least a good being. That's really all I knew.

"Can't Gina…?" Robbie was clutching at straws, and we both knew it.

"Too late," I muttered. "He's gone."

Outside there were lights flashing and a lot of commotion. The cavalry had arrived, or at least a posse of sheriffs and deputies or whatever they had out in the boondocks. It could have been Scotland Yard for all I cared. The Clarks Hill cop must have called for backup. I hadn't even noticed him leaving the restaurant. Maybe he even called them when he first arrived, or maybe all the 911 calls that must have come from the people in the neighborhood alerted the powers that be something huge was going down on White Street. Shame they hadn't arrived earlier. I wasn't sure they'd have been much help, but at least then they'd believe our story. Now I wasn't so sure.

There was some shouting, something about putting hands up in the air. I heard Casey's voice saying something in return, but the words were lost in the wind. It was a good thing Robbie had his arm around me, as I wasn't sure I could stand on my own. The adrenaline rush that came during a fight of this nature had subsided, and now I was very, very tired. And sore. My face burned where Lewis clawed me. Gina, poor thing, had a lot of work to do yet. But I couldn't really think about any of that. I was just thinking about Elton and those beady eyes that seemed to stare up at me accusingly.

I should have been happy we had, for the most part, lived through the battle. I wasn't sure any of us would make it, so why was one death bothering me so much?

I knew the answer. Because he trusted me. Because he felt he owed me. Because I got him into this mess. Because of a rat he decided was a pet, a friend, when it could have easily been a snack for him.

Because deep down he was a hero.

A law enforcement person, dressed in brown, burst into the doorway, gun held before him. "Okay," he shouted, "I want to see hands...."

And then he took in the scene. Brandon Lewis, now a big naked guy who was very dead. Elton, his clothes in tatters and covered in black gore, almost decapitated, with his yellow skin, ridged forehead, and one remaining horn. The waitress, slumped in the corner and missing an arm. I didn't blame the guy for not being able to finish his sentence.

Robbie stepped away from me, and we both raised our hands above our heads. Not that there was much reason, as the deputy or whatever he was seemed to have lost interest in us. He was staring at Elton.

"What the hell has been going on here?" he asked. "Is that real?"

"He was," Robbie said softly.

I looked over at the deputy. There were now other guys in uniforms with guns behind him, just as startled as he was.

"We called him Elton," I said. "I never knew his real name. Probably couldn't have pronounced it, anyway. He was a demon and a damned fine person."

I realized I still had the .38 in my hand, now pointed to the ceiling. I signaled to the deputy to let him know I was going to toss it to the floor. He nodded. The guy was young and pale, barely old enough to shave.

Several uniformed guys came over and cuffed me and Robbie. They weren't rough, just doing their jobs. They really barely took notice of us. We were just side issues. Their eyes kept going back to the demon lying in the middle of the room.

As they led us outside, I glanced back to pay my respects to Elton. Something told me I'd never see him again. "Can you get a blanket or something to cover him up?" I asked.

"Sure," one of the cops said, not unkindly.

Outside more vehicles with flashing lights had arrived. Matthew Elliot was on a stretcher, being loaded onto an ambulance. Some paramedics were huddled over Nick with Casey standing by. One of the cops was talking to Casey, but I didn't think he was listening.

A burly guy in a sheriff's uniform approached me.

"Mind telling me just what the hell has been going on here?" he demanded.

I puffed out some air. "Got a few weeks? I'll explain the whole thing to you."

CHAPTER 21

IN THE end the whole shebang was covered up, as I figured it would be. Carson being there helped tremendously. Once he and Gina hobbled onto the scene, everyone concentrated on him and pretty much left the rest of us alone. Gina pulled me aside while the local law and Carson chatted and did a quick healing spell for my wounded face. She was nearly tapped out, but she gave it all she had. It didn't heal my wounds completely, but at least I could refuse medical treatment and no one would argue the point. After that, everyone ambulatory was hauled off to the Tippecanoe County Jail, and we spent the rest of the night and a good portion of the next morning telling our stories.

Just after lunch a deputy came to tell me I was free to go. I didn't ask questions except to inquire after Daisy.

"The weird-looking dog?" he asked.

I told him yes, and he said he wasn't sure what had happened to her but that he'd check for me. It turned out she was fully recovered and was being looked after by one of the dispatchers.

Nick, Carson, and Matthew Elliot were taken to a hospital in Lafayette. As soon as he was released, Casey went to check on Nick. Gina, Robbie, and I headed back to Indianapolis. Gina went straight to her place, mainly to let Graig and Laura know their exile was over. There was no longer a need for them to remain in hiding. I wondered if Emma would be happy things would return to normal, or if she'd miss the couple she'd been watching over for days now. Something told me it would be the latter.

I needed a week-long shower followed by a month-long nap. I didn't get either, as Robbie got to the bathroom before me and used up all the hot water.

And just as I was about to put my head against a pillow, my phone rang. It was Carson.

"You're sounding chipper," I said.

"That friend of yours knows her stuff. I think she even cured the arthritis in my hand. Now get your butt over here. We gotta talk."

So instead of visiting Morpheus, I drove to Lafayette and chatted with loads of police types in Carson's room at St. Elizabeth's Hospital in order to come up with a plausible cover story. In the end we went with gang warfare, of course. Why a gang war would erupt in the sleepy little town of Clarks Hill was anyone's guess, but that wasn't my concern. And sure, some of the residents would insist they saw wolves roaming the streets, but the night was dark, with storm clouds raging. Easy to see things that weren't really there, right?

Frankly I was too tired to care. When the cop party was starting to break up, I still had one question I wanted answered, so I approached the burly guy who seemed to be in charge.

"What's going to happen with Elton's body?" I asked.

He frowned at me. "Who?"

"Big yellow guy. Covered in black blood. Hard to miss."

The sheriff looked at me like he just wished I'd go away and take all his troubles with me. "I haven't the foggiest idea, to be frank. I mean, he's not human. He's a...."

I'm glad he didn't finish his sentence because it might have lowered my opinion of him.

"Where is he now?"

"Morgue. I've got a man there making sure no one takes a picture of him or anything. The last thing we need is a bunch of pictures of a demon showing up on Twitter or whatever."

"I can see that he's buried."

The sheriff sighed. "There isn't a precedent for this. I don't know what to do." He thought a moment and then shook his head. "Take him. Get him off my hands. Just make sure no one finds out about this."

AND SO three days later, I was standing in a field over an unmarked grave. With me were Robbie, Gina, and Dave Carson. Carson was there because the field was owned by his sister. I didn't know he had a sister. Guess in all the years we'd known each other, it just never came up. But her family lived on a farm outside of the city and had a lot of acreage, and the section we chose for Elton was far from the house and by a little stream. A burr oak stood watch over Elton's final resting place. It was afternoon and a soft breeze was blowing.

Several of Carson's most trusted buddies helped us in digging the grave and depositing the simple coffin. They didn't know who was in the box. Just to help things, Gina helped them forget the whole incident. Me, I'd never forget.

I hated there could be no marker. I hated I didn't even know his real name. I hated I had no idea if he had friends who should be notified of his demise. As they would likely be demons anyway, I doubt they'd be interested in seeing me.

Robbie held my hand as I stared down at the rectangle of earth. Gina was on my other side, softly murmuring prayers. Carson stayed a few steps back, keeping a respectful distance. Close enough to show his support but far enough to give us privacy.

I felt like I should be crying, but no tears fell. Robbie squeezed my hand gently, which helped.

I was feeling guilty, of course. It should be my grave people were standing over, if anyone's. It was my enterprise, my mission. It was my case, my responsibility. Yes, I made sure everyone knew how dangerous it was, and I certainly warned we might not all make it through alive. That, however, didn't help. I still felt guilty. And angry. And very, very sad.

Gina finished her prayers, and we stood in silence for several moments. Finally Robbie said, "He was pretty brave. That's for sure."

I nodded. "He certainly was."

Robbie glanced at me. "Is his spirit…?"

"No. He's moved on."

Carson approached slowly, keeping his head bowed. He patted me on the back.

"I didn't really get a chance to know him," he said, "but he seemed like a good guy."

That brought a slight smile to my face. Elton would have enjoyed being described as a guy.

It seemed like time to leave, although I was reluctant to do so. Robbie released my hand to wipe a tear from his eye. "Good-bye, big guy," he said, his voice cracking a little.

"Take care, my friend," I said. "Somehow I thought we were destined to have quite a few adventures together. I guess maybe in the next life."

Gina made a hand gesture that was almost like a benediction. "Safe journeys, dear companion."

As we walked away, a bird flew over us and landed on a branch of the burr oak. I was glad it was a cardinal and not a crow. It would be quite some time before I could look at a crow again and not feel like I was being watched. The red bird began to chirp, and in my mind, he was singing Elton off to the other side.

"A FAT lot of good I was," Nick moaned. "I got shot two minutes after everything started!"

"It was more like twenty seconds," I said jokingly.

Nick made a sour face. "You're not helping."

We were in Nick's apartment. His cats were chasing each other down the hall. They'd tumble into the living room where we were and look at us like we were interrupting their fun. Then they'd disappear down the hall again, sounding like a herd of buffalo. Every now and then the white cat, Winter, would stop and stare at Casey, hold his gaze for about fifteen seconds, and then go back to cat play. Maybe he was expressing his displeasure at Nick having someone new in his life, or maybe he could tell Casey was a mind reader and was seeing if his little feline brain was being scanned. Who knew?

Nick had put out a bowl of potato chips, and I was doing my best to avoid taking one. No matter the brand, I couldn't stop at one. One hundred, maybe. Best not to give in at all. But damn, that bowl on the coffee table was making my mouth water.

Casey, sitting next to Nick on the couch, seemed to have no trouble with chip addiction. He finished munching his third and patted Nick's leg, which was in a cast. "I thought you did great," he said.

"And how do you arrive at that conclusion?" Nick demanded.

Casey's eyes were mischievous. "You provided distraction so that kid didn't shoot me."

Nick snarled and grabbed a chip. "I've faced ghosts by the score, including one of a serial killer, but I get taken out by some pimply kid with a pop gun! What's going to happen to that little bastard, anyway?"

I gave in. Salt, glorious salt! I'd barely swallowed chip number one before picking out the next two. "Strangely enough he's confessed to killing his family. Maybe without his cronies around, he's developed a conscience." I crammed the two chips into my mouth. Well, one was tiny, so it barely counted. "Now how they're going to explain how he killed three people, making it look like the work of a vicious animal, I have no idea. Luckily that's not my job."

"And Lieutenant Carson?"

I smiled. "Recovering nicely. I went to see him earlier. Mrs. Carson says he's not allowed to go out and play with me anymore, as I'm too dangerous."

Nick let out a hollow laugh. "Truer words were never spoken."

The cats spilled out of the hallway and glared at us as if we were in some way ruining their fun. Then Jasmine gave Winter a whop on the side of the head, and off they went again.

Casey grabbed his fourth chip. I was on about my twentieth. His face was grave as he looked at me. "You know I said I sometimes have premonitions."

"I do recall something like that being said."

He nodded. "This one is different. Generally they're pretty vague. Impressions more than anything else. Lately I've been seeing visions. Each time I get a little more information. I still don't have all the pieces to the puzzle, but one thing is very clear. You're in danger. Someone's out to get you."

"You sort of hinted that before. I figured it was the wolf pack."

Casey shook his head. "No, I'm still getting the feeling. It's not over. I mean, the wolf thing is over, but the danger is still out there. It doesn't have anything to do with Ashley and her wolves."

I shrugged. "I'm always in danger. It's my job."

Nick rubbed his cast-covered leg. I wondered if he had an itch. They could drive you crazy if you couldn't get to them. "Casey spent the night here last night—"

"To look after him," Casey explained. Like I cared if they played doctor.

"—and he woke up from this nightmare. Scared the bejeezus out of me."

"I kept seeing this woman with snakes in her hair." Casey leaned back and put an arm around Nick. This seemed to make the itch go away as Nick relaxed in his boyfriend's embrace. "Like in the movies. One of those Gorgons."

"Yeah," I said. "They're just a special kind of demon. I gather there aren't too many of them left in the world. I killed one not too long ago. She may have been the last of her kind. That's probably what you're picking up. Don't worry about it. She's very, very dead."

Casey shook his head. "This one isn't. I think it's the sister of the one you killed. And she's wanting revenge."

Suddenly the chips didn't taste very good.

GRAIG BETZ and his grandmother insisted on taking me and Robbie out to dinner. I figured Laura would be joining us, but it seemed it was just a family affair. Maud chose the Hard Rock Cafe downtown, maybe because she thought it was the type of place Robbie and I frequented. Little did she know Taco Bell would have been more our style.

The place was crowded and noisy, and we'd been waiting for our food for nearly half an hour and I was running out of small talk. Maud's check for services rendered was in my breast pocket, and as usual, I felt guilty for taking money from a client. After all, she didn't ask for her grandson to become entangled with a pack of werewolves. Still, a cynical private eye had to make a living somehow. For the record I only charged her the bare minimum.

She sipped her water and peered over the rim at me and Robbie. I had the feeling we were being analyzed.

When she set her glass down, she said, "There's a story behind you two that I'd love to hear."

"It's a long tale," I said. "It could take quite a while."

Robbie eyed our waitress, who was just serving a table that had been waiting long before us. "It seems we have time."

I was reluctant to give our history, not because I was afraid of Maud's reaction—I was certain she'd heard quite a lot in her lifetime—but because I didn't want to be overheard. So I said, "Let's just say we've had difficulties in our relationship, which are over now."

"You can feel the love," Maud said, a twinkle in her eye. "It emanates off the two of you."

"Grammy, you're embarrassing them," Graig protested, and indeed I did feel a blush come to my cheeks. Luckily the waitress stopped by our table, looking flustered, and told us it wouldn't be too much longer for our food.

"Sometime before tomorrow?" Maud asked her.

The waitress smiled the smile of an overworked person and said she'd see what the holdup was.

When she'd gone Maud looked at me. "Graig's been telling me some of what has gone on. I don't pretend to understand it all, especially rooms that talk, but I do know I'll never be able to properly thank you for all you've done."

I patted my breast pocket. "All the thanks I need is right here." I thought about pointing out the room itself didn't actually talk and it was an invisible spirit inhabiting said room, but I let it go.

She shook her head and smiled slyly. "Don't try to bullshit a bullshitter, Mr. Andrews. You and your friends have suffered heartache in order to get Graig back to me. I know this."

"It's what we do," I told her. I felt a pang of regret as I thought about Elton. Yes, it was what we did, but it came at a cost.

"Tell me this, Mr. Andrews," Maud said. "Is the world not like we've always assumed it was? Are there horrors that most of us are unaware of? Creatures that lurk in the dark? Was this incident with my grandson"—she placed a hand on his arm for a brief moment—"not an isolated case?"

I thought about lying to make her feel better, but I knew she'd catch me telling a fib, so I said, "Sometimes there are things out in the dark. Things most of us can't even comprehend. But there are also a few people who are able to see them, to know when they're a danger to others. That's where I come in."

"And me," Robbie said with a grin. "And Gina, and Nick, and—"

"She gets the idea."

Maud reached across the table and grabbed my hand with both of hers. "God bless you," she said, so serious I knew not to make a flip retort. She shook her head sadly, not letting go of her tight grip. "But I get the feeling that something horrible is coming, that there's going to be a lot of sadness surrounding you very soon."

"It seems lots of people are having premonitions about me lately."

"Don't take them lightly." She frowned. "There's a dark angel watching over you, ready to strike. The dark angel of death. Please be careful, Mr. Andrews."

I really wished people would stop being harbingers of doom when I was hungry.

I'D NOT met Annalise Carson until recently. Actually I'd not even known her name was Annalise. She was always referred to by Lieutenant Carson as "the wife" or, on occasion, "the ball and chain." She was a few years his junior, but it was obvious while Dave kept law and order out on the streets of Indianapolis, her word was law in the Carson household.

She opened the door for me and Gina with a bemused smile. "Well," she said, "if it isn't Mulder and Scully."

I turned to Gina. "I get to be Scully."

"Bullshit" was Gina's succinct reply.

"He's waiting for you," Annalise said, ushering us in. "He's still in bed, although it's getting harder and harder to keep him there." Was there a knowing look in her eye as Gina passed her? "We went to his doctor today. Seems they can't figure out why he's healing so quickly. The doctor said it was nothing short of a miracle."

"Yes, it's odd," Gina said. "Isn't it?"

Annalise led the way down a short corridor to the bedroom. "I've got to finish the laundry, so I'll let you see him alone. Besides, I have the feeling that I'm not supposed to know what you guys talk about."

"Nonsense," I said. "We'll just be discussing werewolves and witches."

Mrs. Carson wasn't amused, probably because she suspected it wasn't really a joke. "Yes, well, try not to get Dave too excited. The doctor said he's still supposed to have a lot of rest." She rapped twice on the door and called out, "Dave! Frick and Frack are here to see you."

I raised an eyebrow. "I preferred Mulder and Scully."

Carson yelled for us to enter, and Annalise nodded at us before leaving to attend to the household chores. Inside the bedroom, which was darkened due to the curtained window, we found Dave Carson sitting up in bed. There were still a lot of bandages on his face, but considerably fewer than when I saw him in the hospital. Still, I couldn't help but be reminded of Lon Chaney Jr. in the old mummy movies.

Carson grinned, although we couldn't see the whole thing due to his entire left cheek being covered with gauze. He used the remote to switch off *The Price Is Right*. "It's good to see you," he said. I had the feeling he meant it more for Gina than for me. "How's Nurse Nightingale today?"

Gina set her huge black purse on the side of his bed. "She's good. How's the patient?"

"Fit as a fiddle and itching to return to work."

"Don't push too hard. You were hurt pretty bad."

"Darling Gina, I was this close to death, and we both know it." He held his thumb and finger mere millimeters apart. "You saved my life."

"It's what I do."

"You wouldn't have been in danger in the first place if it weren't for me," I reminded him.

"Shut up, Andrews. I've told you a million times now, I insisted on helping out. And I don't regret it one iota. You shouldn't try to hog all the fun yourself."

"It's what I do," I answered.

Carson nodded. "Yes, but don't feel guilty when people around you get hurt. We all knew the risks. God knows you stressed it enough."

"Yes, but—"

"No buts. Do you think Robbie, or Gina here, would be willing to stand back while you take on a world of monsters and demons? I can't believe I haven't stepped in and taken part before now."

"Well, you didn't really know exactly what was going on either."

He narrowed his eyes. "I sort of knew. Over the years. The cases I've been involved in with you. Bodies drained of blood or partially eaten. Hell, a guy got eaten by squirrels, for Christ's sake! I knew there was something supernatural going on. I chose to ignore it and let you handle things. Well, no more. From now on when there's a pack of werewolves in town or you're tracking a vampire or whatever, I want to know."

I relented enough to say, "I'll certainly tell you about it."

"Better." Carson settled back onto his pillows as Gina began to pull out her potions and specially treated bandages to minister to Carson's wounds. He eyed her with a slight smile on his lips. "So you're the same Gina as before? The tall, blond one became, somehow, short and raven haired?"

"Long story."

He gazed around his bed. "I'm not going anywhere."

She ignored him and instead sat at his side so she could get to work. Seeing he wasn't going to get any juicy stories out of Gina, he instead changed the topic. "The big guy, Elton."

"What about him?" I asked.

"Before you got to the restaurant that night, I had a little chat with him. Well, I chatted. He grunted a lot. But he did say a few things. He had a lot of respect for you. Did you know that?"

"I did him a favor recently."

Carson shook his head, but Gina was attending to a bandage on his face, and annoyed, she made him stop moving around with firm hands. "He told me about that," Carson said. "Something about a rat. But I think it was more than that. You allowed him into your life despite the fact that he was a demon. You saw that he was trying to become something more. You gave him a chance. He'd have done anything for you."

I smiled without mirth. "Yeah, he gave his life for me."

Carson started to shake his head again but was stopped by a glare from Gina. "True," he said. "But he wanted to stand with you. It meant a lot to him. He knew the risks, probably better than I did. Hell, all I really knew about werewolves before this came from the movies. Elton knew what he was getting himself into. And he did it proudly. Eagerly even. It made him really happy, if that's the word, that you included him."

I knew Carson was trying to make me feel better, and I knew what he was saying was true. And it did help. A little.

"Thanks, Dave," I said, unable to meet his eye.

"Anytime, asshole," he replied.

ROBBIE AND I were out for an early morning run with Daisy. She had fully recovered from her ordeal, thanks to Gina, and seemed to have even more energy than before. We were at Gustafson Park, and she'd already had breakfast, resulting in two less squirrels in the world, and was now leading us all over the place, scampering here and there with joy. Robbie was doing a better job than me in keeping up, which was fine by me. Running behind the two of them, I was treated to the sight of Robbie's ass as he jogged. He was sweating a little, although less than yours truly, and his tight Shania Twain T-shirt was getting pit stains. His hair was damp and he puffed a little, but damn, he looked good in his black shorts and running shoes. I envied his muscular legs. Mine looked puny in comparison.

Daisy came to a stop to sniff the grass and urinate, and I'm sure Robbie was almost as glad as I was for the respite. Hands on knees, we sucked in air. I may have wheezed a little.

"I'm not in the shape I used to be," Robbie said between gasps.

"Who is?" I stood and wiped sweat off my brow.

There was something mischievous in Robbie's smile as he got down on one knee to tie his left shoe. "I never seem to be able to buy shoes that don't have laces that aren't humongously long," he said. "They keep coming untied. Can you help me out a little here?"

"You need help tying your shoes?"

"Just put your finger here. I want to try a double bow so I don't trip all over myself."

I shrugged and got down in front of him. I should have known he was up to something by his demeanor, but I was surprised to see he'd placed a little black box on the toe end of his shoe. "Um," I said. "What's that?"

With a grin he opened the box to reveal the ring nestled inside. He removed it and held it up to my face. It was a lovely gold band with a design of interlocking circles.

"Duncan Andrews," he said, his eyes twinkling, "would you do me the honor of accepting me as your husband?"

"Holy shit," I said. I had to look into his eyes to make sure this wasn't some elaborate joke. It wasn't.

"Is that your answer?"

"Hardly." I held out my hand so he could slip the ring onto my finger.

"I figured one of us had to make the first move, and it wasn't going to be you."

"I guess I just thought that, in a way, we already were married."

"Yeah, well, this bitch wants it official," Robbie said.

Daisy, wanting to see what the two of us were up to, came up and forced herself in between us, looking first at Robbie and then at me.

"I want to hear the words, dummy."

Damn it all to hell, my eyes actually welled up with tears. "Yes," I said.

"Eloquent as always," Robbie said, unable to keep from being a smartass.

We leaned our faces over the dog and kissed. Daisy must have felt left out because, after a moment, she licked the bottom of his chin. That kind of ruined the mood, so I broke off the kiss.

"I love you," I said, gazing into Robbie's eyes.

"And I love you," he replied.

Overhead there was a dark cloud threatening to obscure the morning sun. For now, though, the day was bright, and nothing could ruin my mood. Robbie and I stood, and we kissed again, this time without interference.

As far as I was concerned, that kiss could have lasted forever.

STEPHEN OSBORNE has been a pizza restaurant manager, a semiprofessional wrestler, and a member of an improv comedy troupe. He now lives in rural Illinois with Christine, a Border terrier mix with a diva complex. In addition to writing, seeing musicals in Chicago, and losing at Monopoly, Stephen sometimes spends cold, shivery nights in haunted locations—just because he likes to.

Facebook: www.facebook.com/stephen.osborne2
Twitter: @southbendghosts
E-mail: leftyIN@yahoo.com

PALE AS A GHOST

STEPHEN OSBORNE

A Duncan Andrews Thriller

Private detective Duncan Andrews's best friend Gina is a witch. His dog is a zombie. And his dead boyfriend, Robbie, is a ghost. So it's hardly any wonder that he uses his connection to the supernatural to help him solve cases. Good thing, too, because Duncan has his hands full. Janice Sanderson, the richest woman in Indianapolis, wants him to find her stripper daughter, Brenda, and another client is having some trouble with a specter haunting her family home. On top of that, Duncan has decided to add dating into the mix, though after Robbie's death, he's not sure he's ready.

When Duncan meets Nick while tracking down a lead on Brenda's boyfriend, he shelves his doubts and agrees to a date. Robbie doesn't make it easy on him, showing up to spoil his chances, but that is the least of Duncan's worries—because one of his clients' husbands is missing and there's a serial killer on the loose—one Duncan fears isn't human.

www.dreamspinnerpress.com

ANIMAL INSTINCT

STEPHEN OSBORNE

A Duncan Andrews Thriller
Sequel to *Pale as a Ghost*

Private detective Duncan Andrews has the home-team advantage when it comes to solving paranormal crimes: His best friend, Gina, is a centuries-old witch. His dog is a zombie. And his boyfriend, Robbie, is a ghost.

Duncan certainly has his work cut out for him with this case. Someone's been using the skull of a powerful wizard to control animals, and whoever it is, they're not out to set up a petting zoo. For Gina, the case hits close to home—she knows just how dangerous it is, since the wizard was her father.

Just when he thinks they&rssquo;re close to breaking the case, tragedy strikes, leaving Gina in a coma. Then, after years as a ghost, Robbie finally decides to move on, leaving Duncan to protect young Ashton Marsh, the victim of several strange animal attacks. Suddenly Duncan is working without his supernatural safety net. Without his friends, can Duncan defeat the power of Eleazar's skull and keep Ashton alive? Or will the struggle for his life end in broken bodies as well as broken hearts?

www.dreamspinnerpress.com

THE SCARLET TIDE

STEPHEN OSBORNE

A Duncan Andrews Thriller
Sequel to *Animal Instinct*

Duncan Andrews, a private detective who specializes in paranormal cases, is back, along with his usual gang. Robbie Church, his boyfriend, is a ghost. Gina, a centuries old witch, is his best friend. And Daisy, Duncan's bulldog, just happens to be a zombie. Odd man out seems to be Nick, a history teacher. He's a normal, living human.

Duncan's latest case leads him to a rock band in Indianapolis called The Scarlet Tide. It doesn't take Duncan long to realize all of the band members are vampires. He sets out to destroy them, but runs into trouble with the charismatic leader of the band, Dominic Hunt. Duncan ends up under Hunt's psychic control, and is forced to examine his relationships with Robbie and Nick, as well as his attraction for Hunt. Can Robbie and Gina help Duncan break Hunt's psychic grip? Is there any hope the vampire can be destroyed once and for all?

www.dreamspinnerpress.com

DEAD
END

STEPHEN OSBORNE

A Duncan Andrews Thriller
Sequel to *The Scarlet Tide*

Duncan Andrews's best friend Gina is a witch, his bulldog Daisy is a zombie, and his boyfriend Robbie is a ghost. Duncan himself is just your average private detective, who happens to specialize in paranormal cases.

Robbie's cousin, Jason, has a problem. The house he's living in is haunted by the ghost of serial killer Dr. Stanley Moore. Duncan thinks banishing the spirit will be an easy task, but when confronted, the ghost nearly kills Duncan.

If that's not bad enough, a witch-hunting group called the Order of Cotton Mather have tracked Gina down and are bent on destroying her. And Robbie and Duncan's relationship may be nearing an end, as Robbie feels he's holding Duncan back from having a lover he can actually touch.

Duncan must rid Jason's house of the evil Dr. Moore, save Gina, and somehow manage to hold onto Robbie in the process.

www.dreamspinnerpress.com